Rebekah – Girl Detective

Books 9 - 16

PJ Ryan

Contents

"Rebekah - Girl Detective" is a short story series for children ages 9-12 with the remaining titles to be published on a regular basis. Each title can be read on its own.

You can join Rebekah's fun Facebook page for young detectives here:

http://www.facebook.com/RebekahGirlDetective

I'd really love to hear from you!

I very much appreciate your reviews and comments so thank you in advance for taking a moment to leave one for "Rebekah - Girl Detective: Books 9-16."

Sincerely,
PJ Ryan

All bundled sets are also available in paperback from Amazon. Check the author page here for the complete listing:

http://pjryanbooks.com/

Current series:

Rebekah – Girl Detective

RJ – Boy Detective

Mouse's Secret Club

Rebekah, Mouse & RJ: Special Editions

Additionally several PJ Ryan titles are now available as audiobooks and you can also find those listed at the page above.

Rebekah – Girl Detective #9

Mystery At Summer Camp

PJ Ryan

Rebekah - Girl Detective #9

Mystery At Summer Camp

Chapter 1

Rebekah had been counting down the days until school ended. It was not because she didn't like school. She did. It was because as soon as the days started heating up and getting longer, she knew that summer was coming. Which meant summer camp. It also meant she would get to spend some time with her older cousin RJ.

"I can't wait, I can't wait," she said to Mouse as soon as school ended.

"Me either," Mouse grinned. He went to the same summer camp she did. "I wonder if they'll have that delicious bread pudding again."

"Ugh," Rebekah shook her head. "That's the only thing I don't like about summer camp."

"Well that's alright, you can give me yours," Mouse laughed.

On the morning they were to leave, Rebekah was so excited that she could barely stand waiting for the bus.

"I can't wait, I can't wait, I can't wait!" she whispered gleefully. Mouse rolled his eyes and sighed with relief when the bus finally arrived. The trip was a long one, taking them from the little town of Curtis Bay to the sprawling woods. When they climbed off of the bus, there were already many kids at the camp. They were all chatting loudly and greeting each other after a year apart. Rebekah waved to a few of the kids that she remembered from the year before, but she was really only looking for one very familiar face. That face was not hard to find, because the boy it belonged to was perched on a branch in a tall tree not far off from the group.

"RJ!" Rebekah shouted happily and waved to him. Mouse waved eagerly too and they both ran over to the older boy. RJ was eleven, which made him practically a grown up in Rebekah's mind. He was her cousin, and each year they went to the same summer camp together. RJ had taught her a lot about being a detective, because he was an official Junior Detective. He mailed away for a kit and everything. The year before he showed Rebekah the magnifying glass and fingerprinting set that had come in the kit. He even had his very own badge.

RJ had red hair, just like Rebekah, but he always wore a detective hat, even when he went swimming!

"Hi there!" RJ grinned as he jumped down from the tree branch to greet them. "I've been waiting for you guys all morning," he gave his cousin a quick hug and patted Mouse on the back. When he did, a little white mouse poked its nose up out of Mouse's pocket. It wiggled its whiskers at RJ.

"Aha, I see that you have brought one of your pets," RJ said nervously. He was not a big fan of mice.

"Don't worry," Mouse said with a grin. "This is Magellan. He's supposed to be a famous explorer, but really," he whispered his next words. "He's a scaredy-mouse!"

Mouse was right, because his little pet dove right back into his pocket the moment he saw all of the commotion around him.

"Are you ready for a great summer?" Rebekah asked cheerfully as she, RJ, and Mouse walked toward their cabins.

"It's great to be back in the fresh air," RJ said, and then lowered his voice. "And out of the dangers of the city."

"Dangers?" Mouse asked with a squeak.

"Oh yes," RJ nodded. "There have been many mysteries for me to solve this year."

"We've been solving mysteries too," Rebekah said proudly, and Mouse nodded.

"You must always be careful," RJ warned. "Detective work is best left to professionals," he showed her the badge he had clipped to his belt.

Rebekah nodded, but she felt a little sad. She knew she was a good detective and she wanted her cousin to know that too.

Chapter 2

Mouse and RJ were staying in a boys' cabin, while Rebekah was staying on the other side of the campfire, in a girls' cabin. She was sad to have to stay alone, but there were a few girls she knew from the year before and some nice new friends to make too. However, as soon as they had their things settled, RJ and Mouse came running over to her cabin.

"There's going to be a sing-a-long!" Mouse said happily.

RJ rolled his eyes. "Kid stuff."

Rebekah frowned. She loved the sing-a-long. Did that make her too much of a kid? As they gathered in the bleachers around the campfire, they were all chatting with one another. It wasn't until a few minutes passed that the campers began to realize that there was no one waiting to lead them with the singing. In fact, there were no counselors around at all. Then suddenly in the center of the campground there was a big burst of smoke. It seemed to come from nowhere!

"What was that?" Rebekah shouted as she stood up. RJ stood up right beside her and they both looked ready to investigate. But when the smoke cleared, the sound of a guitar filled their ears. Where no one had stood a moment before, was a man dressed in a counselor's outfit with a guitar slung over his shoulder.

He began to sing the camp song. All of the kids in the bleachers were so shocked by the scene that they didn't sing along. The man who had long blonde hair and brown eyes with a big smile continued to sing as if he didn't care if none of the students sung along.

Mouse, who was staring with wide eyes and an open mouth began to clap loudly. Soon the other kids began to clap too. Rebekah was the first one to start singing, then the other kids, except for RJ of course, joined in. When the song was over the counselor introduced himself.

"My name is Louis, and I am a new counselor here this year. I'll be in charge of entertainment. We'll be having lots of campfires, and even a play, and a magic show."

"A magic show!" Mouse squealed and could barely keep from jumping up and down on the bleachers. Mouse was a big fan of magic and was hoping to be a magician himself one day. "This year is going to be great!"

RJ sighed. "Great, singing, acting and magic. Where's the fun in that?"

"I think it'll be fun," Rebekah said firmly. "But I bet we don't get through the summer without stumbling over a mystery or two."

"I hope so," RJ grinned. "I have a lot to teach you little cousin."

Chapter 3

After the sing-a-long was over, the three began exploring the campground. There was not much new to see, as they had been attending the camp for a few years. But Rebekah found the bird's nest she had spotted the year before, and it had new baby birds in it. Mouse found the little cage he had made out of twines and branches for the last mouse pet he had brought along, right where he left it.

"Are you sure he can't get out of there?" RJ asked suspiciously as he peered into the cage.

"The last one didn't," Mouse shrugged.

RJ glanced up from the cage and noticed something glittering in the leaves ahead of them.

"What's that?" he wondered. When he stepped closer and brushed the leaves away he discovered that it was a sparkly guitar pick.

"Weird," Rebekah frowned. "What would a guitar pick be doing all the way out here?"

"Maybe someone dropped it on a hike," Mouse suggested.

"Maybe," Rebekah said thoughtfully. "We should bring it back to the camp and see if anyone lost it."

"Sure," RJ nodded, but he was staring at the pick. As they walked back to the camp the sun was setting. It was time to share a meal and then head back to their cabins for the night. At dinner they were treated to hamburgers and french fries, a celebration of their first night at camp. After dinner they told a few ghost stories around the campfire.

"That's not possible," RJ muttered to Rebekah when one of the kids told a story about a zombie.

17

"Maybe it wasn't really a zombie, but somebody dressed up like a zombie," Rebekah pointed out.

"Good thinking little cuz," RJ said with a grin. "You get smarter every time I see you."

Rebekah went back to her cabin with a grin on her face. She was so proud of the compliment her cousin had given her that she forgot entirely about the guitar pick they had found in the woods.

Chapter 4

Early the next morning Rebekah heard a knocking on the door of her cabin. Most of the other kids in her cabin were still sleeping. She walked sleepily to the door and found Mouse standing on the other side.

"Rebekah something terrible has happened!" he announced.

"What is it?" Rebekah asked with a gasp.

"Mr. Louis is gone!" he said in a whisper. "He's disappeared!"

Rebekah stepped outside of the cabin still in her pajamas and closed the door. She looked Mouse directly in the eyes.

"What do you mean he disappeared?"

Mouse sighed and started again. "I got up early this morning because I wanted to ask Mr. Louis if I could help him with his magic show. But when I knocked on the counselor's cabin, they said that Mr. Louis was gone."

"What do you mean gone?" Rebekah pressed with frustration.

"Well," Mouse hesitated. "They said he must have gone home, they hadn't seen him after the sing-a-long yesterday."

"Oh Mouse," Rebekah sighed. "Going home is not exactly the same thing as disappearing, is it?"

"No," he frowned. "But Rebekah I don't believe it. Didn't you see how excited he was yesterday about putting on all the shows? Why would he just decide to leave?"

Rebekah frowned too, it did seem strange. "Well maybe he had an emergency. Or maybe he realized how many mosquitoes are in the woods!" she smacked her arm sharply as a mosquito made a feast out of her.

"I don't think so," Mouse shook his head. "Rebekah, I know I'm not usually the one who finds the mysteries, but I have a feeling about this one."

"And what feeling would that be?" RJ asked from just behind them. He had woken up early to investigate some sounds he had heard the night before outside of his cabin.

"Mr. Louis is gone," Mouse explained quickly.

"Maybe the Bertha got him," another voice said. It was a kid even older than RJ. He was going to blow the bugle to wake everyone up for the morning when he overheard their conversation.

"Who's Bertha?" RJ asked.

"You've never heard of Bertha?" the boy asked with a chuckle. "She's the bear that lives in these woods."

"What?" Rebekah shook her head. "I've never heard of any bear living in these woods."

"Oh," the boy lowered his voice. "That's because you're just kids. They don't want to scare you. But my big brother was a counselor here, and he told me all about Bertha. She's a giant bear and every once in a while she gets hungry."

Rebekah shivered at the thought. Mouse glared at the boy and RJ tapped his chin thoughtfully.

"Well, if the bear were big enough," he shrugged.

"Mr. Louis did not get eaten by a bear!" Mouse said and stomped his foot against the dirt. "This kid is just trying to scare us. Aren't you?" he asked.

"Well," the older boy shrugged. "I guess until you see her for yourself, you'll never believe me!" with that he stalked off to the microphone that he would blow his bugle into.

"Do you think he might be right?" Rebekah asked quietly.

"No way," Mouse said sternly.

"Well, it is the woods," RJ pointed out. "If this were the city, I wouldn't think so, but there are a lot of animals that live in the woods."

"Listen, Mr. Louis is gone and we need to find him," Mouse said firmly. "I don't care if it was a bear or an alien, but we need to find out what happened."

RJ sighed heavily and shook his head. "Mouse aliens aren't real."

Mouse rolled his eyes and stalked off across the campground.

"I'm going to find him with or without your help!" he called over his shoulder.

"Don't worry Mouse, we'll help!" Rebekah called after him. She looked back at her cousin to see if he was coming too, but saw that he was staring at something in his hand. She noticed the sparkle. It was the glittery guitar pick they had found in the woods the day before!

"Oh no," Rebekah said quietly.

"Oh no is right," RJ agreed as he held the guitar pick up into the air. "I think Bertha might just be involved after all."

"Maybe he just dropped it," Rebekah pointed out.

"Why would he have been all the way out in the woods though?" RJ asked. "It seems a little strange to me."

"Me too," Rebekah agreed. "Come on…let's tell Mouse we're on the case!"

Chapter 5

"Mouse, wait!" Rebekah shouted as she chased after him.

"What are you kids doing running around camp?" a counselor asked as she spotted them. "You should be getting in line for breakfast."

"But, we have to find-" Mouse began to say.

"You don't have to find anything until after breakfast," she said sternly. "There are dangers in the woods, you can't just go running off like this. You guys have been here before, you should know the rules."

"I'm sorry Ms. Cindy," Rebekah said quickly. "We just thought that we saw something in the woods."

"Yes," RJ said as he looked at the counselor. "And I heard some strange noises outside of my cabin last night."

"It was probably just squirrels," Ms. Cindy said. "There are lots of squirrels around here."

"You don't think it could have been a bear?" RJ asked boldly and tilted up the brim of his hat.

"A bear?" Ms. Cindy laughed and shook her head. "I think you three have heard too many scary stories. Go back to your cabins, get dressed and be at breakfast in five minutes or no swimming today!"

She walked off toward the dining hall.

"See, no bears," RJ shrugged as he turned toward his cabin.

"Don't you think that's what any grown up would tell a kid?" Rebekah pointed out. "Remember that boy said they didn't want the little kids to know about it."

"Well," RJ shrugged. "I'm not a little kid."

Rebekah frowned as she ran off to her cabin to change out of her pajamas. Once she was dressed she met Mouse and RJ for breakfast. Mouse was wiggling around in his seat.

"Hurry up and eat, we have to find out what happened to Mr. Louis."

"And how are we going to do that?" RJ asked.

"There has to be a way to prove that he's missing and that he didn't just leave," Rebekah said thoughtfully.

"We have this," RJ said and laid the sparkly guitar pick on the table.

"But we don't even know for sure if it belonged to him," Rebekah pointed out. "The counselors are not going to believe us with just that. We need to find some proof."

"You're absolutely right, little cuz," RJ nodded. "You really are getting good at this detective work."

"Thanks," Rebekah beamed.

Mouse sneaked some of the cheese from his egg sandwich to the mouse in his pocket.

"But how are we going to get proof? What proof might there be?" Mouse asked.

"Well, RJ heard noises outside of your cabin, so maybe it was the bear. If it was the bear, it should have left proof behind," she smirked.

"Oh gross, I'm not looking for bear poop," Mouse said sternly.

"No, ugh," Rebekah groaned. "I meant footprints!"

"Paw prints," RJ corrected smugly.

"So it's agreed?" Rebekah asked hopefully. "As soon as we can, we'll get away from the activities and see if we can find any bear tracks," she glowered at RJ.

It was not easy to get away from the counselors as the first full day of camp was packed with activities. But one hour was set aside for nature time, and the campers were allowed to explore the woods as long as they did so in groups and didn't go past a certain point. As soon as they were allowed to go into the woods, Rebekah, Mouse, and RJ doubled back and headed for the boys' cabin. They walked around behind the cabin searching through the grass and fallen leaves for any sign of a bear.

"I don't see anything," Rebekah frowned.

"I do," RJ sighed as he pointed to a family of squirrels running up and down a nearby tree. "Ms. Cindy was right and that must have been what I heard after all."

"Great," Mouse frowned. "Now how will we find Mr. Louis?"

"Maybe we should go back to where we found the guitar pick," Rebekah said. "If it is his, maybe we can find some tracks there."

"Bear tracks?" Mouse asked nervously.

"Maybe, or maybe Mr. Louis's tracks," she said.

Chapter 6

The three moved through the woods as quickly and quietly as they could. They were past the boundaries the counselors had set and if they were caught, they would be banned from swimming and even campfire activities. When they reached the part of the woods where they had found the guitar pick, RJ held up his hands.

"Now everybody freeze. Until we know what happened to Mr. Louis, this is officially a crime scene. There could be evidence all over the place!"

He whipped out a magnifying glass that had also come in his detective kit and began looking over the leaves on the ground.

"I'll look for claw marks on the trees," Mouse suggested.

Rebekah had her eye on something else. She had noticed a broken twig in the middle of some crushed leaves. She crouched down beside it and looked at it more closely. Not far from it she saw something in the dirt.

"Look!" she cried out happily. "Look what I found!"

The two boys ran over to her to see what she had discovered. It was a shoe print.

"So if it belongs to Mr. Louis, then he wasn't attacked by a bear," Mouse said with relief.

"But just what was he doing out in the woods, alone?" RJ asked suspiciously. "Doesn't seem like a normal thing for a counselor to be doing."

"Well, let's find out!" Rebekah said as she began to follow the footprints. They led a little further into the woods and then down a trail. The trail was very overgrown with bushes. It looked as if no one had walked down it except Mr. Louis in quite some time.

"Where was he going?" Mouse asked with confusion.

"Ouch!" Rebekah frowned as a thorn in one of the bushes scraped her arm. "Doesn't seem like a nice walk in the woods, that's for sure."

The trail ended at the edge of a clearing. There was nothing but dirt and a few shrubs to see. But there were no more footprints!

"How is this possible?" RJ muttered to himself as he inspected the dirt closely with his magnifying glass.

"He couldn't have just stopped walking," Rebekah whispered.

"Unless," Mouse said hesitantly.

"Unless what?" RJ asked as he and Rebekah looked at him.

"Unless he was carried," Mouse said sadly. "By a Bertha."

RJ and Rebekah exchanged worried frowns at Mouse's words. As much as Rebekah didn't want to believe that a bear had carried off Mr. Louis, she also couldn't see another explanation.

"Well somehow he stopped making footprints," Rebekah shook her had.

"But there aren't any bear tracks either," RJ pointed out. "There's no tracks at all, except our own."

"Well that's great," Rebekah suddenly said. "That means we've solved our mystery!"

"What?" RJ said with surprise.

"How do you figure?" Mouse demanded.

"We wanted to find Mr. Louis and we have," Rebekah said sternly. "A person can't just disappear. So Mr. Louis has to be here somewhere."

"Maybe he turned into a squirrel," Mouse suggested with a shrug.

"Really?" RJ asked with an arched brow.

"Mouse," Rebekah sighed and smacked her forehead. "He's not a squirrel."

"So you're saying he has to be here somewhere," RJ said softly. "Well maybe he didn't turn into a squirrel, but he might have climbed a tree."

They all took turns looking as high up into the trees around them as they could, but there was no sign of a camp counselor who thought he was a squirrel.

"If he's not in the trees, then where is he?" Rebekah said with frustration. She knew that they had already been gone far too long. Soon the counselors would come looking for them, and all they had for an explanation for breaking the rules was a glittery guitar pick. Mouse sat down on a large fallen tree limb and sighed.

"No one is going to believe us and poor Mr. Louis will never be found."

"What if there isn't anything to believe?" RJ pointed out. "So far all we found for evidence was some foot prints, that may not even belong to Mr. Louis."

"That's true," Rebekah nodded. "But I think Mouse is right. Something tells me Mr. Louis is in trouble and we need to find him."

"Hunches are important," RJ nodded. "But they're not everything Rebekah, you need some real evidence to back them up."

Mouse sighed heavily again. He slumped forward, resting his elbows on his knees. When he did, his mouse escaped the front pocket of his shirt. It went running across the dirt.

"Ah!" RJ shrieked and jumped up into the air as the mouse scuttled by his feet. "Get that thing! Get it, get it!" he demanded as he jumped up and grabbed a low tree limb so that he could get away from the mouse.

"Relax it's just a little mouse," Rebekah couldn't help but giggle.

"I don't like mice!" RJ grumbled as he continued to swing from the tree limb. Mouse had jumped up to chase his little friend.

"Come back here!" he demanded as he ran after the mouse. "I've already lost Mr. Louis, I can't lose you too!"

Chapter 7

As Mouse ran after his pet, they all heard voices calling out through the woods.

"Oh no they're looking for us!" Rebekah winced. "We are going to be in big trouble."

"And we didn't even find Mr. Louis," RJ shook his head.

Rebekah knew if she didn't call out where they were, they would be in even more trouble. So she shouted to the searchers.

"We're here, we're okay!"

As soon as the words were out of her mouth she heard a loud thump. She spun on her heel to see that Mouse had chased his pet into some thick brush at the edge of the trail. But the thump had not come from him running into bushes, that was for sure!

He rubbed his forehead. "Ouch," he muttered.

"What happened?" RJ asked.

"I don't know," Mouse shook his head. "There's something behind the bushes."

"What?" Rebekah asked curiously and started to pull the bushes back. All three of them began tugging at the branches and leaves. Soon they found that the bushes had grown up around an old wooden shack.

"Wow!" Rebekah announced when she felt the wood under her fingertips. "I never would have known this was here."

"Look, that must be where my mouse went," Mouse said as he pointed to a small hole in the bottom of the wooden shack. "We have to get inside! I can't leave without him."

The counselors were getting much closer, and Rebekah knew that they wouldn't be happy that Mouse had brought a pet with him. They would make him go back to his cabin without his friend. She couldn't let that happen to Mouse.

"Alright, let's see if there's a way in," Rebekah said quickly. They pulled harder at the bushes until they found a door.

"This must be it," Rebekah said as she tugged at the wooden handle on the front of the door. But the door wouldn't budge. A large thick branch of the bushes was pinning the door shut.

"Hello?" a voice called out from inside the shack. "Hello is there someone out there?"

Rebekah, Mouse, and RJ all froze at the sound of the voice.

"Do you think that's Magellan?" Mouse whispered.

"No silly," Rebekah laughed. "It must be Mr. Louis! Mr. Louis, is that you?" she called out into the shack.

"Yes it is!" Mr. Louis called out. "Oh please help me get out, I've been stuck in here all night!"

Rebekah, RJ, and Mouse teamed up to tug at the branch. They pulled as hard as they could and were able to get the door part of the way open. Mr. Louis gasped as light spilled into the dark shack that he had been stuck inside of.

"I'm so glad you kids found me," he said. He began pushing back against the door as they pulled, in an attempt to get the door all the way open.

"This isn't working," RJ frowned. "We need to all push together!"

All three wedged themselves inside the door one by one, so that they could push with all their might against the door with Mr. Louis. But while they were pushing hard, the branch of the bush was pushing back just as hard.

"Can you get out Mr. Louis?" Rebekah asked through gritted teeth.

"No, I'm sorry," Mr. Louis sighed. "You are much smaller than me, I can't fit through there!"

RJ lost his footing in the loose dirt, and knocked accidentally into Rebekah who lost her footing too. As they tried to get their balance, they weren't leaning their weight against the door anymore. With only Mouse left to push on the door along with some help from Mr. Louis the door snapped shut once more.

"No, no!" Rebekah cried out as she tried to shove her weight against the door again, but it was too late. When it closed, it trapped all of them inside! In the shadows of the shack, all three kids and Mr. Louis groaned at their situation.

"Now how will we get out?" Mr. Louis sighed.

"We'll find a way," Rebekah said with determination. Mouse was busy looking around the shack.

"What are you looking for?" RJ asked.

"For Magellan!" Mouse replied as he searched the floor of the shack.

"Oh no that mouse is in here with us!" RJ gasped. He began dancing from one foot to the other.

"Mr. Louis what were you doing in here?" Rebekah asked as she shoved on the door, hoping that it would open.

"Well I wanted to put on a really special magic show for you guys, and I had heard rumors about this shack being out here. I thought if I found it, maybe I could use it for a disappearing act," he frowned.

"Well you sure did!" Mouse laughed as he scooped up a squeaking squirming mouse and dropped him into his front pocket. RJ sighed with relief.

Mr. Louis nodded. "I pried the door open, but it slammed shut before I could stop it, and then I couldn't get back out."

"Now we're all stuck," Mouse pointed out with a sigh.

"Hey, where did you kids go?" Ms. Cindy shouted from just outside the shack. The counselors were still looking for them!

"Come on everyone," Rebekah said quickly. "Let's make as much noise as we can!"

They banged on the wooden frame of the shack and shouted at the same time.

"We're in here! We're in here! Under the bushes!"

Chapter 8

The counselors soon discovered the hidden shack. They worked together to pull the branch of the bush that held down the door free. When the door swung open, Rebekah, RJ, and Mouse stepped out, followed by Mr. Louis.

"Louis, what are you doing in there?" Ms. Cindy asked with surprise. "We all thought that you went home early!"

"Luckily for me these kids came looking for me," Mr. Louis said with a shake of his head. "Otherwise I might have been stuck in that shack for a very long time."

"Well Louis," Ms. Cindy said with a frown. "We have rules at this camp you know. We follow the buddy system for a reason!"

Mr. Louis nodded with a sigh. Rebekah was surprised that Mr. Louis was the one getting into trouble. She held her breath as she wondered if they would be next.

"And as for you three," Ms. Cindy said as she crossed her arms and stared at them. "Well you're just regular heroes! Thanks to you Mr. Louis is safe! You should be very proud of yourselves."

Rebekah beamed, as did Mouse. But RJ only shrugged.

"Well I am a junior detective, after all," he said with a slight huff.

"You three have been so brave, I'll make sure I tell the cook to give you each extra desert!" Ms. Cindy announced happily.

"Fantastic!" Mouse said happily.

"Great," Rebekah cringed. She wondered just how much bread pudding Mouse could eat.

That night at dinner, Ms. Cindy announced to all of the campers and other counselors that Rebekah, Mouse, and RJ had rescued Mr. Louis.

"We should all give them a round of applause!"

All of the other campers cheered and clapped for them. Rebekah felt very proud. Mouse barely noticed as he was too busy with three dishes of bread pudding in front of them. RJ smiled at Rebekah and gave her a thumbs up.

"Good work little cuz," he said. "We make a great team!"

At the end of the week, Mouse and Mr. Louis had another treat for the campers. They put on the greatest magic show ever.

"Now, I will make this little mouse disappear," Mr. Louis announced and waved his magic wand over Magellan.

"I don't care where it goes, as long as it stays away from me!" RJ cringed. Rebekah laughed and waited with everyone else to see just where Magellan would show up.

"Oh dear," Mr. Louis said as he lifted the box and discovered that there was no mouse underneath. "It seems our little mouse might be missing," he sighed dramatically. Rebekah suspected it was all part of the act. RJ pulled his feet up on to the bleachers. Then his eyes widened.

"Rebekah," he squeaked. "Is my hat moving?"

Rebekah looked up at his brown detective hat and gasped. It was indeed wiggling back and forth on his head.

"Ah!" RJ cried out and snatched his hat off of the top of his head.

"There he is!" all the kids cheered.

"Don't worry RJ, I'll save you!" Rebekah declared. She scooped Magellan up out of his thick red hair. "See, no more little mouse," she grinned.

"My hero!" RJ sighed as he sat back down.

Rebekah couldn't have been prouder.

Rebekah - Girl Detective #10

Zombie Burgers

Chapter 1

The pen could not have moved any faster across her notebook. She kept scribbling away. Rebekah was sitting at her usual lunch table. She had it reserved since the first grade. She was watching the new cook in the cafeteria who was limping as she walked between the tables. It was Rebekah's third day as a fourth grader, and already she felt much smarter. Especially since she was the only one to discover that the new lunch lady was a zombie. There was no question about it. Rebekah scribbled another note as the cook walked the line of food. She moved very slowly. Whenever she walked she stumbled a little. At one point she almost lost her balance and let out a long low groan.

Rebekah added to her notebook: Walks like a zombie, Groans like a zombie.

She tapped her pen lightly as the other students around her happily ate their meals. Rebekah hadn't touched her food. Her stomach was churning over the idea of the lunch lady being a zombie. The only thing she couldn't figure out was why would a zombie want to work in a school cafeteria? What could she be after? Maybe she was hiding out, and trying to blend in. Or maybe she was out for something tasty, that wasn't on the lunch menu, like brains! What better brains could there be than brains of kids in school? They were active and growing kids walking from classroom to classroom. She imagined they would have to be pretty tasty to zombies.

Brains? Rebekah scribbled down in her notebook.

"Brains?" Mouse asked as he sat down beside her with a frown. "What is that supposed to mean?"

Rebekah glanced up at her best friend, and narrowed her eyes. Out of the top pocket of Mouse's shirt a little white mouse stuck out its tiny pink nose.

"Nothing," she said and wrapped her arm around her notebook. She didn't want him to see.

"What is it?" he asked more firmly. "Let me see!" he tugged at her arm and tried to catch a glimpse of what she had written.

"Fine," Rebekah said and pushed the notebook toward him with a huff. As Mouse read over her notes, his eyes got wider and wider. Rebekah continued to tap the pen, this time on the table. She watched as the woman walked back toward the kitchen. Mouse looked up at the woman she was watching and shook his head.

Chapter 2

"Her name is Mrs. Rosado, and she is not a zombie," Mouse said confidently.

"How do you know?" Rebekah asked.

"Because I met her on the first day. I always ask for any leftover cheese for my mice, and she was very nice. She said she would save it for me," he smiled. "What kind of zombie would save me cheese?"

"You didn't see, what I saw," Rebekah pointed out.

"No, no! School just started Rebekah, our books won't even open all the way yet, you can't be accusing the lunch lady of being a zombie!" he smacked his forehead and groaned.

Rebekah cleared her throat. "On the first day of school I saw her walking funny down the hall."

"Most grown ups walk funny," Mouse pointed out. "They're always wearing weird shoes."

"Well I, being the courteous person I am, followed her to offer some help, since was having a hard time," Rebekah explained.

'Of course," Mouse nodded slightly.

"Well she went to a side door near the kitchen. She opened it. There was this man that I've never seen before," Rebekah said.

"Okay, well there are a lot of men in the world," Mouse shrugged.

"This man was very pale," Rebekah explained in a lowered voice.

"Lots of people are pale Rebekah," Mouse sighed.

"He also wore very old clothes," Rebekah said.

"Lots of people wear old clothes too," Mouse interrupted, getting frustrated.

"Oh really, well do lots of men walk off across the field of the school with their arms held out like this?" Rebekah stretched her arms straight out in front of her. When she glanced up she saw Mrs. Rosado staring at her. She dropped her arms quickly back to her sides.

"Seriously?" Mouse asked. He had no explanation for why someone would be walking across a field like that.

"So, she's a zombie," Rebekah said with a nod. "Probably the queen zombie!"

Mouse shook his head fast from side to side. "No! She's not a zombie!"

Rebekah met Mouse's eyes and smirked. "Prove it."

Mouse sighed and nodded. "Alright, I'll show you. We'll spy on her. You'll see she's not doing anything in the kitchen but making food."

"Eat your food children!" a voice said from right behind them. Rebekah nearly jumped out of her chair when she looked over her shoulder and saw that it was Mrs. Rosado. She opened her mouth to speak, but all that came out was a little squeak.

"Yes ma'am," Mouse said with a charming smile. Mrs. Rosado moved on to the next table. Once all of the students were done eating their food Mouse and Rebekah hung out near the kitchen door. Mrs. Rosado was busy preparing lunch for the next day. She was dumping lots of hamburger meat into a big bowl.

"Yum, burgers are my favorite!" Mouse whispered to Rebekah. Just then they both heard a grinding sound. It was very loud. Mrs. Rosado stepped back into view carrying the pitcher from the blender. It was filled with a green frothy substance, almost like a goo.

"Uh, what is that?" Rebekah asked and scrunched up her nose.

"She's not going to-" Mouse started to say as Mrs. Rosado walked up to the bowl of hamburger meat. Before he could finish his sentence Mrs. Rosado dumped all of the green goo into the hamburger meat. Mouse was horrified and nearly slumped over in shock. Rebekah held his arm to keep him standing. Mrs. Rosado laughed as she stirred the hamburger meat.

"They'll never even know," she smirked. She glanced in the direction of the kitchen door. Rebekah and Mouse ducked out of the way swiftly. They were out of sight just in time.

"Let's get out of here," Mouse groaned. "I think my tummy is upset."

"Mine too," Rebekah narrowed her eyes. "What are the chances of having a zombie for a cook?"

"Now wait," Mouse said with a frown. "We still don't know for sure that she's a zombie. We need to look back at our evidence."

"You're right," Rebekah agreed and pulled her notebook out of her pocket. Together they looked over the list of evidence that they already had.

"She talks to zombies," Rebekah said.

"Or a man that look like a zombie," Mouse pointed out.

"She walks like a zombie," Rebekah said.

"Or she wears funny shoes," Mouse reminded her.

"And now, she put zombie goo in the hamburger meat!" Rebekah declared.

Mouse opened his mouth, but then he shook his head. "That one I can't argue with."

"So what are we going to do about it?" Rebekah asked with a scowl.

"What can we do?" Mouse sighed and glanced over his shoulder in the direction of the cafeteria. "It's not like anyone is going to believe us. Just in case she is a zombie, we probably shouldn't make her mad by accusing her. So what can we do?"

Rebekah narrowed her eyes thoughtfully. "Well we have to do something!" she announced.

Chapter 3

That afternoon when she got home from school, her mind was filled with ideas of how to stop the zombie. Maybe she could make a zombie trap. Maybe she could find a zombie hunter that specialized in such things.

One thing she knew for sure was that she couldn't sit by while Mrs. Rosado pretended not to be a zombie. In fact, she had to wonder why a zombie would want to work in a school lunch room. What was she planning?

Rebekah could barely eat her dinner. She kept thinking of that green goo. Would it hurt the students? Had she sneaked it into other meals at school? When she went to bed that night, Rebekah was still trying to figure it out. Of course Mrs. Rosado was a zombie, but why would a zombie be a lunch lady? It just didn't make sense.

Rebekah fell asleep thinking of this. Sometime during the night she heard a tapping. At first it was a tapping, and then it sounded more like a scratching. She woke with a start and looked at her window. The curtains were drawn. There was a long shadow behind them. It looked like an arm that was reaching for her window. Rebekah was scared, but she had to see what it was. She held her breath as she crept over to the window. She grabbed the edges of the curtains and closed her eyes tightly.

"Please don't be a zombie, please don't be a zombie," she said under her breath. All at once she pulled the curtains back. The tapping and scratching wasn't from a zombie at all. It was a branch from the tree beside her window. But there was a zombie! At least, what looked like zombie! A zombie with wild red hair and wide scared eyes.

"Oh no!" Rebekah gasped. "It's me!" It was her reflection in the window that she had thought was a zombie.

Tired from not sleeping all night, Rebekah's face was very pale. She crawled back into bed, her mind still spinning with fear. That's when she realized what Mrs. Rosado was up to. She wasn't there to cook food for children. She was there to turn the children into an army of zombies!

Chapter 4

When Rebekah arrived at school the next day she was more determined than ever to put a stop to the zombie lunch lady. She had the entire school to protect! Mouse caught up with her in the hallway just before class.

"Hi Rebekah," he said cheerfully. His smile faded when he saw her scowl. Even the mouse in his pocket ducked down to avoid it. "I guess we're still thinking the lunch lady is a zombie," he sighed.

"Not only is she a zombie," Rebekah said as she slammed her locker shut and began marching down the hall. "She's trying to turn all of us into zombies too! That's what that goo was!"

Mouse frowned as they entered their first class of the day. "Well it is strange that she would try to hide it from everyone."

"Settle down class," the teacher announced from the front of the room. "Please listen to the morning announcements."

The PA system squawked to life and a tinny voice carried through the speakers.

"Today's lunch will be a special treat, hamburgers and french fries!" the voice announced. Rebekah and Mouse looked at each other with wide eyes. The tinny voice went on to list the clubs that would be meeting after school.

"I told you!" Rebekah hissed at Mouse. "What kind of school lunch doesn't even have vegetables?" she pointed out. "It's all a big trick to make us eat the hamburgers."

Mouse nodded slowly. "I think you might be right about this one Rebekah. But aren't we in over our heads? Maybe we should call your cousin RJ?"

Rebekah shook her head as she folded her arms. "No way. We can handle this ourselves."

"But how?" Mouse asked.

"All I know for sure is that no one is going to eat those hamburgers today!" Rebekah said sternly.

Mouse nodded as if he agreed, but he looked a little worried too. Rebekah always had a way of getting them both into trouble with her detective work.

Chapter 5

At lunch time, Rebekah marched into the cafeteria. She was determined to stop the students from eating the hamburgers. She knew that one bite might be the last real meal they ever had. Once they were zombies who knew what they would eat. As she looked around at all the children milling about, excited about having hamburgers and french fries for lunch, she felt bad for them. They were going to miss out on a delicious treat. But it was for their own good. Rebekah walked boldly up to the lunch line. Mrs. Rosado was standing behind the counter ready to serve her zombie hamburgers.

"I know what you did," Rebekah hissed at her. Mrs. Rosado raised an eyebrow.

"Excuse me?" she said. "What did I do?"

"I'm not going to let it happen. I'm going to stop you. So you might as well whip out the peanut butter and jelly sandwiches right now!"

Mrs. Rosado gritted her teeth and took a deep breath as if she was trying very hard to be patient.

"Would you please move along and collect your food. Other students are waiting," she pointed to the line forming behind Rebekah.

"Do not eat these hamburgers!" Rebekah announced to the line of students. But they weren't listening. They smelled the french fries and the toasted buns. They pushed past Rebekah ready to feast.

"Oh no!" Rebekah gasped. She had really thought that the other kids would listen to her. She expected they would line up behind her and march right out of the cafeteria in protest. But apparently eating french fries was more important than not becoming a zombie! Rebekah tried to grab the attention of the kids leaving the lunch line with their tray.

"Don't eat it!" Rebekah pleaded. "She put zombie goo in it! It will turn you into a zombie!"

Most of the kids seemed to think that Rebekah was joking. Or maybe that she had somehow gone insane. They all just laughed at her and carried their trays to their tables. Mouse entered the cafeteria just as Rebekah was going into a full panic. He saw the wildness in her eyes and braced himself for what might happen next. Soon the lunch room tables were filling with trays and students ready to eat. Things were getting out of control and fast. Rebekah could only think of one thing to do. She went to the fullest table and stood in front of it.

"This is for your own good!" she promised the students who stared at her with confusion. Rebekah jumped up on top of the table, knocking off trays and cartons of milk as she did.

"No one eat the burgers!" she shouted again and again. "No one eat the burgers, they're no good! They are filled with goo!"

Mrs. Rosado came running out from behind the counter to see what was happening.

"Oh no!" she shrieked when she saw the mess that Rebekah was making. "What have you done?" she demanded.

"I told you I would stop you," Rebekah said with a smirk as she jumped from table to table. She kicked off all the trays with hamburgers. The kids were staring at her in horror as they all tried to guess just how much trouble she would be in. Mouse hung his head and tried to disappear. He hoped that Rebekah wouldn't expect him to jump on the tables now. Mrs. Rosado chased after Rebekah the best she could with her limp.

"Stop that," she shouted as Rebekah kicked off another tray. "Stop that right now!"

Rebekah jumped on to another table before the lunch lady could catch her. She sent all the trays scattering from one end of the table. Someone must have gone to fetch the principal Mr. Powers, because it was his voice that boomed across the cafeteria.

"Stop this nonsense right now!" he shouted. Rebekah ducked and turned to face him. She was obviously the guilty party, since she was standing on top of a lunch room table.

"Get down this instant," Mr. Powers snapped as he folded his arms across his chest. Mrs. Rosado smirked as Rebekah reluctantly climbed down off of the table.

"Young lady, it is the fourth day of school, isn't it?" Mr. Powers asked with a raised eyebrow.

"Yes sir," she said solemnly.

"We couldn't get through one week without a food fight?" he asked sharply.

"It's just the hamburgers–" Rebekah started to say.

"In my office, now," he said sternly and then looked at the other students. "I'm sure that Mrs. Rosado can provide each of you with a nice peanut butter and jelly sandwich. You may eat out on the playground, just for today, since the cafeteria will need to be cleaned."

Rebekah received quite a few glares from the other students. They had all been looking forward to their hamburgers and french fries.

"Let's go," he said to Rebekah and marched out of the cafeteria. Mouse waved slightly to Rebekah who sent him a frown that made it seem as if she was doomed.

Chapter 6

Mr. Powers' office was very neat and tidy. Everything had its place. Even Rebekah who sat down right in front of his desk.

"Now Rebekah," Mr. Powers said sternly. "I understand if you feel strongly about being a vegetarian."

Rebekah's eyes widened, but she did not correct him, she only nodded her head.

"Yes Mr. Powers," she said with a frown.

"I'm not a big fan of meat myself," Mr. Powers said with a shrug. "But you can't expect everyone else at the school to follow your same diet. Okay?"

"Yes sir," Rebekah said shifting in her chair. "So I'm not in trouble?"

"Well I can't have you making a scene like you did today again, young lady," the principal warned. "But I think if you go and help Mrs. Rosado clean up the mess you made that I can let you slide this time."

Rebekah shuddered at the idea of having to be alone with the zombie lunch lady, but she nodded. "Yes sir," she said. At least she wouldn't be getting a detention.

As she stood up from her chair and walked toward the door of the office, she spotted a man walking down the hallway. He was very pale, and wore old and dirty clothes. She knew she was supposed to go back to the cafeteria, but she couldn't let a zombie wander the school!

She followed after the man through the empty hallways. When she saw him pause beside a utility closet she ducked behind a bank of lockers. The man glanced around once and then unlocked the door. He stepped inside of the closet.

Rebekah ran up to the closet and peeked inside the small window. She wanted to know what he was doing in there. Was he storing the zombie goo for Mrs. Rosado? Was he hatching some other terrible plan? To her surprise, there was no one in there!

How could he have just disappeared? Was he a zombie ghost? A zombie magician? She had no idea what to think. But she was sure that if she didn't get back to the cafeteria and help Mrs. Rosado she would end up in detention after all. She ran down the hall back toward the cafeteria, her mind brimming with explanations for the zombie's disappearance.

When she walked back into the cafeteria it was empty, except for Mrs. Rosado who was leaning over picking up some of the trays that Rebekah had knocked over. As she stood up she let out a loud groan that made Rebekah want to run right back out of the cafeteria. But she knew that the principal would never believe her.

"You," Mrs. Rosado said with a glare. "You clean up this mess!" she said sternly and then stalked back into the kitchen. As Rebekah was cleaning up the trays and the food from the floor she thought about the hamburger meat. She knew that Mrs. Rosado had made a lot more. She was sure that the next day she would be serving hamburgers again. She couldn't let her turn the entire school into zombies. As Rebekah put the last tray back on to the counter, she called out into the kitchen.

"I'm all done!"

Mrs. Rosado came out to inspect her work. As she was checking under the tables for any stray french fries, Rebekah ducked into the kitchen. She found the bowl of hamburger meat and tossed it out in the garbage. Then she slipped back out.

"Fine," Mrs. Rosado said with a huff. "Don't do that again!" she insisted. "You may not like my cooking, but it is very rude to make such a scene. It is even worse to try to cause all of the other kids to feel the same way."

Rebekah nodded, her heart pounding. "I'm sorry," she said through gritted teeth. She hoped Mrs. Rosado wouldn't notice the hamburger meat was thrown out while she was still there. "Go to class," Mrs. Rosado instructed. She placed her hands on her hips and watched as Rebekah left the cafeteria. Rebekah could feel her zombie eyes on her back the entire way.

Chapter 7

Rebekah ran all the way to her next class. It had already started, and the teacher waved her inside. He tried to hide a smirk of amusement. He had heard about her antics in the cafeteria. Mouse was waiting there for her, her desk saved so that she could sit next to him. She slumped down at the desk, her features creased by a frown.

"I can't believe how brave you were," he whispered to her once she was settled.

"I don't know about brave," Rebekah shivered as she recalled the feeling of zombie eyes watching her. "But luckily I didn't get detention."

"How did you manage that?" Mouse asked with surprise. He was certain she would have a year's worth of detention.

"Mr. Powers thinks I'm a vegetation," Rebekah giggled behind her hand. Mouse rolled his eyes and shook his head.

"Good one Rebekah," he mumbled.

When class was over it was almost time to go home. They began walking down the hallway toward their lockers to gather what they needed to take home.

"I was thinking," Mouse said with a frown. "If she really is making some kind of zombifying concoction, maybe we can get a sample of it to check it out in the science lab."

"Then we would have evidence!" Rebekah said cheerfully. "Mouse you really are brilliant!" she hugged him tightly.

"I know," Mouse laughed. "Now let go, or you'll squish Boyardee!"

"You named your mouse, Boyardee?" Rebekah asked with surprise.

"Well I found him behind some cans of spaghetti-os," Mouse started to explain and then shook his head. "No time for that, we need to find a way to prove what Mrs. Rosado is up to."

"So how are we going to get a sample?" Rebekah wondered.

"Well if we wait until after the last bell rings for the day we can sneak into the kitchen," Mouse suggested.

"I like the way you think," Rebekah grinned. They hurried off to their last class of the day.

Chapter 8

After the last bell rung they met up in the hall outside of the cafeteria. "Are you ready for this?" Rebekah asked him.

"As ready as I'll ever be," Mouse replied with a nervous smile. "Hopefully she's already gone home for the day."

They leaned around the corner of the kitchen door. The kitchen was empty. They slipped inside and began searching through the kitchen for any of the green goo.

"Ugh look," Mouse said as he pointed to the blender that had a little bit left in the bottom.

"There's our sample," Rebekah cringed at the smell. Just then the kitchen door creaked as if it was about to open. Mouse and Rebekah looked around searching for anywhere to hide. The only option was under the curtained sink. They squished together in the small space and held their breath as the door swung all the way open, with a loud groan. Mouse closed his eyes and Rebekah pushed her head back as she tried to hide. It had to be Mrs. Rosado. They heard her footsteps dragging along the floor as she walked over to the sink. The water turned on for a moment. Then off. Then they heard chopping.

"Get back here you," they heard her hiss. "They won't even know what they're eating, but these kids need a good dose of Mrs. Rosado's special recipe," she giggled shrilly. Then she grew silent for a moment, before adding along with a sharp chop. "Well you're a slimy one, aren't you."

Chop! Chop!

Rebekah cringed and wondered just what she might be slicing up. What went into zombie goo? She wasn't sure, and she did not want to find out. Mrs. Rosado limped away from the sink. They hoped that she had left, but a moment later they heard the grinding of the blender.

"She's making more!" Rebekah hissed. "Our lunches will never be safe!"

Mouse nodded quickly, his face growing pale at the very thought of that green goo being inside of his hamburger. When the grinding stopped, they both waited. Rebekah wished the woman would just leave. Didn't she have other zombie duties to attend to?

"I think she might be gone," Mouse whispered beside Rebekah's ear.

"Are you sure?" Rebekah whispered back, feeling very worried that they might walk into a trap.

"Only one way to find out," Mouse replied quietly. He began to pull aside the curtain on the sink. Rebekah winced, hoping that they would not be caught. Before Mouse could even get the curtain all the way open, Boyardee slid out of his shirt pocket. It was easy for the mouse to do because Mouse was leaning over, looking for the lunch lady's shoes.

Chapter 9

"No Boyardee!" Mouse hissed. "Come back here you bad mouse!"

But the little white mouse was just a blur as he bolted across the kitchen floor. Suddenly they heard a shriek.

"A mouse in my kitchen?" Mrs. Rosado fumed. "Never!" they heard her limping quickly after the mouse.

"No, no," Mouse sobbed. "She's going to turn Boyardee into a zombie mouse!"

Rebekah frowned. She knew how much Mouse's mice meant to him. She also knew that a zombie mouse would not be nearly as fun. Bravely she stepped out from under the sink to rescue the mouse. All of Mrs. Rosado's shrieking and hollering had reached the ears of her zombie friend. When Rebekah stepped out from under the sink they were both chasing the mouse.

"Leave that mouse alone!" Rebekah declared loudly.

"You again!" Mrs. Rosado threw her hands up into the air. "Why are you doing this to me?"

"Why am I doing this to you?" Rebekah asked with surprise. 'Why are you doing this to us? Why did you have to pick our school for your army of zombies?"

Mrs. Rosado stared at her as if she had sprouted a carrot out of the top of her head. She shook her head slowly.

"Say that again?" she asked.

"I said, why did you have to pick our school to create your army of zombies?" Rebekah repeated and then shot a glare in the other zombie's direction.

"Why would you ever think I was making an army of zombies?" Mrs. Rosado asked, so dumbfounded that she couldn't even be angry.

"Well, let's just see why," Rebekah said sharply. She whipped out her detective notebook and began to read off the list of evidence. Meanwhile Mouse started hunting for Boyardee.

"You walk like a zombie," Rebekah explained. "You groan like a zombie, you talk to zombies," she pointed at the man standing beside Mrs. Rosado. "You created a zombie goo to sneak into our food-"

"Zombie goo?" Mrs. Rosado said with a short laugh. Then her eyes lit up. "Do you mean this?" she asked as she picked up the blender pitcher filled with frothy green goo.

"Yes that," Rebekah said and then covered her mouth with both hands. She made noises behind her hand that sounded like, 'I won't drink it'.

"This is not zombie goo," Mrs. Rosado said with another laugh. "This is vegetables," she pointed to the broccoli, peppers, celery, and cucumbers that she had used to create the concoction. "I just thought it would be a good way to make sure that all of you kids were getting a good helping of vegetables each day," she explained with a trembling smile. "I can't believe that you thought I was a zombie!"

"What about your limp and your groan?" Rebekah asked, still not convinced. Mouse walked up beside her with Boyardee captured in his hands.

"Yes, and this zombie," Mouse pointed at the man beside Mrs. Rosado. "Rebekah saw him walking with his arms straight out in front of him."

"Mr. Baker is not a zombie either," Mrs. Rosado said sternly. "Now listen, I think it's great for kids to have imaginations, but you two take the cake with this one. I have a limp because my back is bad, and I groan and moan because sometimes when I lift things or bend over, it hurts."

"And I am the new groundskeeper and janitor for the school," Mr. Baker said with a shake of his head. "When you saw me, I was doing a special exercise for my arms. I spent a lot of time in the basement this past week stacking and emptying boxes so my arms were sore. Mrs. Rosado taught me an exercise that her doctor taught her, to help with her back."

Rebekah sighed as all of the pieces of the puzzle began to come together. Mr. Baker was pale because he worked in the basement so often. "And I guess the entrance to the basement is in the utility closet?" Rebekah asked with a grimace.

"Yes it is," he nodded slightly. "How did you know that?"

"I might have followed you," Rebekah said quietly. "I might have thought you were a zombie ghost because you disappeared in the closet."

"A zombie ghost," Mr. Baker laughed at that. "Well you are a creative one."

"So just to be clear," Mrs. Rosado said with a point of her finger. "I am not a zombie and neither is Mr. Baker."

"Yes ma'am," Rebekah said quietly.

"Yes ma'am," Mouse agreed. "But I still don't want vegetable goo in my hamburgers!"

"Are you going to tell Mr. Powers?" Rebekah asked nervously. She knew that he wouldn't be so nice with a second offense.

"Hm," Mrs. Rosado said. "I'll make you a deal. If you two promise not to tell the other kids what I sneak in their hamburgers, then I promise not to tell Mr. Powers about this little incident."

Rebekah nodded solemnly. "It's a deal," she said.

As Rebekah and Mouse started to walk out of the kitchen, Mrs. Rosado called after them.

"And keep that mouse out of my kitchen!"

Rebekah – Girl Detective #11
Mouse's Secret

MICE ONLY

PJ Ryan

Rebekah - Girl Detective #11
Mouse's Secret

Chapter 1

Rebekah was sprawled out across her bed, flipping through a new book that her cousin RJ had sent her in the mail. It was a book all about famous detectives throughout history. Rebekah thought of herself as a girl detective. Her cousin RJ was a detective too and he was always on the look-out for tips and advice to share with Rebekah. So far the book was interesting, but it was very thick. It had a lot of pages and Rebekah couldn't understand some of the words. She jotted down the ones she didn't know on a pad of paper so that she could look them up later.

As she read through the stories, she imagined being back in time with these detectives. She could be their trusty assistant. It would have been very interesting to solve mysteries before there were cameras, computers, and telephones. As she flipped to the next page she heard a strange sound. It was a scampering sound. It made her a little nervous. It reminded her of monster claws or the little feet of gremlins.

She sat up on her bed and pulled her feet up on to the bed with her. Bravely, she looked in the direction of the scampering sound. A white blur bolted across the floor of her bedroom. Rebekah's eyes widened and she gasped.

"Mouse!" she called out, but she wasn't yelling at the small white rodent that was now hiding under her bed. She was calling out to her friend Mouse, who she suspected was hiding in the hallway.

"Hi Rebekah!" he grinned as he stepped into her room. Mouse always had a pet mouse with him. He had over twenty mice of his own. He liked to collect them and give them different names. That was how he got his nickname, Mouse. Rebekah had called him that since the first day they met and a mouse had run across her shoe.

"Get him!" Rebekah said as she jumped down from the bed and began searching underneath it for the mouse. "If Mom sees him she will have a fit," she giggled at the thought.

"Don't worry," Mouse smiled as he crouched down and held out a small piece of cheddar cheese. The mouse scampered right out from under the bed and into the palm of Mouse's hand.

"Wow, he's hungry," Rebekah laughed as the mouse scarfed down the entire piece of cheese in a matter of seconds.

"What are you up to today?" Mouse asked. It was Sunday so they had the whole day to play.

"I was just reading," Rebekah shrugged as she held up the book about detectives.

"Nice," he said with a smile. "Did RJ send you that?"

"Yup, but I am ready to take a break," Rebekah grinned. "What are you up to today?"

"I was hoping we could go to the park, I brought my soccer ball," he pointed out into the hallway where a green and black soccer ball was waiting for them.

"Great!" Rebekah grabbed her shoes and put her book carefully on her desk. "And don't forget we have our bowling night on Wednesday," she said quickly as she caught sight of her bowling bag in the corner of her room. She and Mouse had a Wednesday night tradition of going bowling together.

"I won't forget!" Mouse promised. Then she and Mouse ran down the stairs and out of the house.

Chapter 2

Rebekah and Mouse walked down to the park that was not far from where they lived. It had a big grassy field as well as a playground. On the grassy field people would play ball, fly kites, and sometimes do cartwheels and gymnastics. It was a fun place to be, especially on a sunny day.

As Rebekah and Mouse began kicking the ball back and forth, some other kids came over to play too. They all had a game of kick-away which was a lot of fun. In kick-away everyone has to try to kick the ball away from the person who has it. Then whoever kicks it away and gets to it first is the one that everyone else has to kick the ball away from.

There was no way to win really. It was just a way to have fun and it always made everyone laugh and shriek as they tried to kick the ball away. When the other kids had to leave and it was just Mouse and Rebekah again they began tossing the soccer ball back and forth.

"I'm really glad that we came to the park," Rebekah said with a smile.

"Even though there are no mysteries to solve?" Mouse asked with a lop-sided grin.

"Oh there are mysteries," Rebekah said firmly with a glimmer in her green eyes. "There are always mysteries. But it's my day off!"

They both laughed. When Mouse threw the ball toward Rebekah, he caught his foot in a thick patch of grass. He started to fall, so the ball went high over Rebekah's head. Mouse caught himself with his hand, but his pet mouse slipped out of the top pocket of his shirt. The mouse scampered along the grass toward the woods. The ball was rolling in the other direction. Mouse chased after his pet, while Rebekah chased after the ball.

"I'll get it!" she called out and tried to run faster. When she snatched up the ball, she turned around in time to see Mouse chasing his pet right into the woods.

"Do you need help?" she offered.

"I'll get him!" Mouse called over his shoulder as he disappeared into the woods.

Chapter 3

Mouse could easily see his pet as he chased after it. Its white coloring made it stand out against the green and brown leaves that were scattered across the ground in the woods. But catching it was not as easy. The mouse was fast, that's why Mouse had named it Speedy.

"Come back Speedy!" he called out and reached into his pocket for some extra cheese. Mouse and Rebekah had rules to follow while they were at the park. One of those rules was not to go into the woods alone. But Mouse hadn't planned on going so far into the woods. He thought he would catch his pet right away.

He realized as he chased down his mouse that he was getting deeper into the woods than he had ever been before. Finally he caught up with his pet who was burrowing in a pile of leaves. He scooped Speedy up into his hands and dropped him into the front pocket of his shirt. As he did a pine cone knocked him right on the top of the head.

"Ouch!" Mouse growled and glared up at the tree. Of course, the tree hadn't meant to throw a pine cone at him, at least he didn't think so. There was something strange about the tree however. In its branches it looked like something large had been built. It was molded all around the tree. It looked a bit like a small house or a very large tree house.

"It's a tree house!" he gasped and stared up at it with admiration. He had always wanted to build one, but his yard had bushes and not so many trees. It looked like the tree house hadn't been used in some time, but there was still a rope ladder dangling from a branch that would let him climb up and go inside.

"Mouse?" he could hear Rebekah calling for him. He knew if he didn't go back soon she would be worried enough to come looking for him. Then she might get lost in the woods! He wanted to climb up to take a look at the tree house, but he didn't have time at the moment. So as he walked back to the edge of the woods he tried his best to remember exactly how he had gotten to the tree house. Once he stepped outside of the woods, Rebekah was there waiting for him.

"Are you okay?" she asked. "I was about to come look for you."

"I'm fine," Mouse said quickly. "Speedy is fast!"

"Good name then," Rebekah laughed.

Mouse was just about to tell Rebekah about the tree house, when suddenly he didn't want to. He wanted to be the first to explore it. Rebekah was such a good detective, and she always found everything first. He wanted to have the tree house to himself, just for a little while.

To take his mind off of it, he decided to practice one of his new magic tricks.

"Hey did I show you that new magic trick I learned?" he asked with a wide smile. Mouse was very good at magic tricks. Well, he tried to be very good at magic tricks. He wanted to be a magician. He liked the idea of tricking people into believing that something amazing had happened. He was always learning new tricks from books or websites on the computer.

"No you haven't," Rebekah said reluctantly. Rebekah didn't really like magic tricks. She liked mysteries that were meant to be solved, not mysteries that were meant to fool you.

"Oh great, well let me show you!" Mouse said eagerly. He always liked to show off his magic.

"If you must," Rebekah frowned and stood impatiently in front of him.

"Oh," Mouse frowned. "You don't want to see it?"

"Well, I was having fun playing soccer," Rebekah explained as she held up the ball in her hands. "I was hoping we were going to keep playing."

"It won't take long," Mouse promised her. "I think you're really going to like it."

"Mouse," Rebekah shook her head slightly. "You know I don't really like magic tricks."

"Trust me, you'll like this one," Mouse insisted. He began pulling out a long ribbon of cloth from his pocket. Rebekah groaned as that was one of the oldest magic tricks in the books. "What? Did I already show you?" Mouse asked with a confused frown.

"No, but I've seen it before," Rebekah shrugged. She wasn't impressed. Rebekah was always very up front about how she felt, and Mouse knew that she didn't mean to hurt his feelings, but she did. He was upset that she wouldn't just watch one trick.

"Fine," he said sharply. "Forget about it," he shoved the ribbon back into his pocket.

"Great, let's go play!" Rebekah said quickly. She had no idea that she had actually hurt Mouse's feelings.

"No, forget about that too," Mouse said sternly. He took the soccer ball from her. "I'm going home."

"Oh," Rebekah was surprised. "I thought you wanted to play some more?"

"No, I'm going home," Mouse repeated and then stalked off out of the park with his soccer ball tucked under his arm. Rebekah stared after him. She wasn't sure what to think. But she didn't even consider that she might have hurt Mouse's feelings.

Chapter 4

The next morning at school Rebekah waited for Mouse by his locker. They usually met up before classes. But she didn't see him. When the bell rang she had to go to class. She caught glimpses of him during breaks between classes, but he was always walking in the other direction.

The next day at school Mouse didn't meet her at his locker. He also didn't meet her for lunch. She was getting very upset, thinking that he was trying to avoid her. She had never had a hard time finding Mouse before.

At the last bell she stalked right out of school to look for him. She found him around the side of the school near the bicycle racks. He was talking very quietly with a few other kids. Rebekah knew them from school.

There was Amanda, who Rebekah knew from art class. There was also Max who she knew from gym class, and Jaden who she had seen in the lunch room. They were all gathered around Mouse who seemed to be whispering.

As Rebekah got closer, Mouse stopped talking. He looked at her and then turned his head. Rebekah gasped. Mouse had never snubbed her before. What was he talking to the other kids about?

Rebekah was just about to walk over there to find out exactly what was happening, but before she could get over there, Mouse and his friends began marching away. Rebekah was going to call out to him but she knew that he had seen her. She knew that he had decided that he didn't want to talk to her.

Her feelings were very hurt, but more than that, she knew that this was a mystery. She had to find out why Mouse was avoiding her. She had to find out what they had been talking about.

Chapter 5

When Rebekah got home from school, she decided to pay Mouse a visit. She was going to get the truth out of him, even if he was angry with her. So she marched her way to his house. She marched up his sidewalk. She marched up to his front door. Then she knocked on the door.

She was practicing in her head exactly what she would say to him. She would remind him of what good friends they were. She would remind him that she didn't like to be left out. Most of all she would remind him about their bowling night, which was coming up fast. But it wasn't Mouse that opened the door. It was Mouse's mother.

"Oh hi Rebekah," she said with a smile. "Are you looking for Mouse?" she asked.

"Yes I am," Rebekah said firmly, but she had to smile politely at Mouse's mother.

"Well he's already gone to the park," his mother said. "I'm sure he will meet you there."

Rebekah had her feelings hurt all over again. Mouse had gone to the park, their park, without her? Why wouldn't he have invited her to go?

"Thanks," she said sadly, and turned away from the door. She walked toward the park with her shoulders slumped. She couldn't think of a single reason why Mouse would leave her out.

As she got closer to the park, she noticed a group of kids walking in front of her. It was the same kids that she had seen earlier in the day and Mouse was leading the way. Not only had he left her out of going to the park, he had invited all of his new friends instead!

She hung back far enough that they couldn't see her. Then she crept along the bushes and the trees that lined the sidewalk. She followed them until they entered the park. She watched as they skipped the playground. They walked across the grassy field without stopping to play tag. They walked right to the edge of the woods.

Rebekah gasped as she saw Mouse lead the other kids into the woods. The rule was that they were not supposed to go too far into the woods, but Mouse just kept walking. Rebekah knew that she would be seen if she walked right behind them. So she entered the woods from closer to the playground. She had to listen very closely to the sounds of their voices and footsteps. With the crunching of the leaves she could tell which direction they were walking in. When she got closer she spotted something strange. There were pieces of cardboard taped up on the trees. They were signs. Some of the signs said: Keep Out! No Entry! Mice Only!

Rebekah was sure that Mouse was up to something very strange now. When she sneaked closer to the voices, she saw just how strange. One by one, each of the kids was climbing a rope ladder up a very large tree. Mouse was the last one to get all the way up. When she looked up she saw that the ladder had led to a big tree house.

Chapter 6

Rebekah sat there for some time and waited for them to come down. She heard snippets of laughter. She heard voices back and forth. She didn't hear anyone calling down to her to come up.

As she walked home she was very upset. But she did not let herself cry. She would not. Mouse was obviously under some kind of mind control. Or maybe he had been invaded by an alien body snatcher. Either way, she was going to get her best friend back no matter what it took.

That night as she laid awake thinking about what might be going on with Mouse, she made a plan. She would evaluate Mouse for signs of being brainwashed. She knew him well so that she should be able to tell. So she made a list of three signs that she would look for.

Does Mouse have one of his mice?

Does Mouse have a new magic trick?

Does Mouse remember their secret handshake?

She fell asleep sure that she would be able to reveal the truth.

Chapter 7

The next day as soon as she got to school she started looking for Mouse. He wasn't easy to find. He wasn't at her locker. He was at Jaden's. She waited until Jaden had gotten his books and walked away. Then she caught up with Mouse as he turned to walk toward class. He almost walked right into her. When he looked up at her, his eyes were wide.

"H-hi," he stammered.

"Hello Mouse," Rebekah replied, her eyes narrowed. She crossed her arms over her chest and stood right in front of him. "How are your little mice?"

"Fine," he gulped. A small white mouse poked his head up out of Mouse's pocket. Rebekah frowned. She was sure that if he was brain washed he wouldn't remember to bring his pet to school with him. "I have to go now," he said quickly. He hurried away from her in the hallway before she could even say another word.

Rebekah dragged her feet all the way to class. She slumped down at her desk. She pulled out her notebook and crossed off the first test.

When the bell rang she rushed out into the hallway. She ran up and down the hall looking for Mouse. She thought at first she wouldn't find him, but then she spotted him. He was standing near the water fountain. He was whispering to Amanda. Rebekah was not shy about walking right up to Mouse this time. Amanda smiled at her as she walked past. Rebekah glared. She looked right at Mouse.

"So Mouse, do you know any knew magic tricks?" she asked, arching one eyebrow very high.

"Of course," Mouse said with a surprised smile. "Do you really want to see it?"

"Sure," Rebekah shrugged. She didn't like magic too much, but she wanted to make sure that this really Mouse and that he was in control of his own thoughts.

"Look at this," he whipped out a bright red rose. Rebekah could tell that it was not a real flower. But she played along anyway.

"Oh is that for me?" she asked.

"No, but you can smell it," he said and held it beneath her nose. Rebekah sighed and sniffed the flower. She expected it to turn into a piece of cloth, or maybe to split into two flowers. What she did not expect was a face full of water sprayed from the center of the flower.

"Mouse!" she shrieked as she wiped at her face and sputtered. "What is that? That was no magic trick!"

"Sure it is," Mouse laughed. "It's just a different kind. It's a magic trick with a joke!"

"Oh great," Rebekah said dryly. Even though she was wet she was glad that Mouse was talking to her. She fell into step beside him as they began walking to their classes.

"Mouse I really thought-"

"Rebekah, I have to go," he said quickly and ducked into his classroom. Rebekah stared after him with surprise. It was not even time for the bell to ring. She knew he didn't have to go into class that fast. Now she was really hurt. She was more than hurt. She was mad. If he didn't want to be friends with her anymore, all he had to do was say so. She marched off to her own class, fuming.

Chapter 8

As Mouse sat in his class he started to feel very bad. He knew that Rebekah probably didn't mean to hurt his feelings, even if she had. By the time school was over he decided it was time to forgive her. He waited for her outside of school. When Rebekah walked down the sidewalk, she stomped right past him as she was still upset.

"Rebekah," Mouse called out as he ran to catch up with her. "Are you doing anything this afternoon?"

"Oh just go be with your new friends," she snapped without stopping.

"Rebekah," Mouse frowned as he realized how much he must have hurt her feelings. "How about we go for ice cream, just you and me?" he said with a bright smile. Rebekah didn't want to agree. She wanted to stay mad, but she missed Mouse. He was really her best friend.

"Alright," she finally nodded. As they walked to the ice cream shop, Mouse told her about the new magic tricks that he had learned.

"So these tricks are still magic tricks, but they wind up being more like practical jokes," he laughed.

"Well if they're anything like that squirting flower, you can keep them," Rebekah said firmly.

What she really wanted to know about was the tree house she had seen in the woods. But she didn't want to upset Mouse when they were just laughing together again. She decided she would ask him about it when they went bowling the next night.

After they finished their ice cream, they both had to head home to study for the science test they had the next day. As Rebekah tried to study, she found it nearly impossible to concentrate. She really wanted to know the story behind the tree house. More importantly she wanted to know why she was not invited to be part of it.

She was still very happy that she and Mouse were talking again. As she fell asleep that night she began dreaming of the bowling alley. The only problem was, the pins were all made out of mice! Every time she rolled the ball down the alley, the mice would scatter.

Chapter 9

Rebekah woke up feeling excited the next day. She and Mouse were supposed to go bowling that night. She hurried to dress, brush her teeth, and grab her breakfast.

When she got to school she didn't see Mouse at his locker, so she just went to her own. He wasn't at lunch and this made her quite mad. She wondered if she had done something wrong. Did she order the wrong kind of ice cream? Did he know that she was rolling bowling balls at mice in her dreams?

She soon brightened up when she aced her science test. She was looking forward to sharing the news with Mouse.

When she couldn't find him after school she went to look for him by the bicycle rack. Again, he wasn't there. She was getting more and more frustrated. It was like he was avoiding her all over again. As soon as she got home she called his house.

"Hello?" Mouse answered as if nothing was the matter.

"Hello?" Rebekah replied with annoyance. "Where were you all day?"

"Oh, just a busy day," Mouse said quickly.

Rebekah frowned. She doubted that was true. "Well are you ready to go bowling tonight?" she asked.

"Oh no!" Mouse gasped. "I forgot that was tonight. I'm sorry Rebekah but I'm just too busy. I won't be able to go."

Rebekah was shocked. Mouse never missed one of their bowling nights.

"What are you busy with?" she demanded but Mouse was already hanging up the phone. "I'll find out the truth!" she insisted just before the phone cut off.

Chapter 10

When Rebekah hung up the phone, she had had enough. She was not going to let this fly. She was going to find out exactly what Mouse was up to once and for all. She grabbed her notebook, and flipped it open. There was one last test. Their secret handshake, which they hadn't used in years, but Mouse should still remember. They used it whenever they got into a fight, to show that all was forgiven.

She put her bowling ball bag back in the closet and stomped out the door. She knew just where Mouse would be, and why he was too busy. She was sure that if she got to the tree house first, the ladder would be down. But as she walked toward the park, someone zipped right in front of her. It was Amanda, with her hair streaming out behind her, riding her bike. She waved to Rebekah as she headed for the park.

Rebekah knew that if Amanda got their first she would never be able to sneak into the tree house. So she began to run, hoping to beat her somehow. As she began to run someone came flying out of a yard and on to the sidewalk. Rebekah almost ran right into Jaden.

"Oh sorry!" he said, and jogged off in the direction of the park. Now Rebekah had to catch her breath. She was getting pretty frustrated. She couldn't give up, even if she wanted to. She had to find out what was going on. Just as she reached the edge of the park she caught sight of Max running across the grassy field. Now she knew she would be too late. Her shoulders drooped as she walked across the field and into the woods. She could hear them all talking together ahead of her.

"Isn't this going to be great?" Amanda giggled.

"I can't believe it took this long," Max replied.

"What a big surprise!" Jaden laughed.

Rebekah pouted. She wanted to know what they were talking about. She felt very left out, which made her angry and sad at the same time. All of the sudden she remembered when all of this had started. She remembered the look on Mouse's face when she didn't want to see his magic trick. This whole time she had been thinking that Mouse was the one who was being mean, but really she had started it!

"Oh no," Rebekah muttered as she realized that she had hurt Mouse's feelings. He hadn't been brainwashed, or had his body taken over by aliens, he had just been hurt. Rebekah sure knew how that felt now. She decided that if he forgave her, she would always want to see his magic tricks. Hopefully, it wasn't too late.

When she reached the tree house she was sure the ladder would already be pulled up. But instead it was dangling down against the tree. She looked up at the tree house and saw that it was dark. Maybe they hadn't gone up there? Maybe they were meeting somewhere else? Rebekah decided to check it out anyway. As she climbed up the ladder she wondered what might be inside. Just as she reached the top, lanterns turned on inside of the tree house. Rebekah peeked inside the door to find Mouse, Jaden, Max, and Amanda, huddled inside.

Chapter 11

They all smiled at her and cheered.

"Welcome to the club Rebekah," Mouse said with a wide grin.

Rebekah was very surprised. "But, I thought you didn't want me to be in it?" she said nervously.

"Rebekah if there's one thing I know, you'll always solve a mystery," Mouse laughed. "I knew you'd hunt me down tonight, so we planned a special celebration."

He pointed to the snacks and drinks covering a small table in the tree house. "All this is to welcome you to the club. That is, if you want to be in it," he added.

"Of course I do!" Rebekah said and held out her hand with her thumb folded down against her palm. He held out his hand the same way. Then they intertwined their fingers and shook twice. Then their thumbs popped out and thumb wrestled. Rebekah won!

"I'm sorry I hurt your feelings Mouse," Rebekah said with a frown.

"I know you didn't mean to," he said with a shrug. "I'm sorry I left you out. But now you can be part of Mouse's Secret Club."

"And what exactly is that?" Rebekah asked suspiciously as she crunched on a potato chip.

"You'll have to stick around to find out," he grinned and winked lightly at her. Rebekah laughed and shook her head.

"As long as you don't squirt me with any more flowers!"

"Well," Mouse grinned as he and the other kids exchanged secretive looks. "I might."

Rebekah sighed and sat down on the floor of the tree house. "Alright, tell me all about it!" she said as cheerfully as she could.

"Well, when I found this tree house I was really excited," Mouse explained as he sat down beside her. "I came up to check it out. I figured it would be full of spiders and bugs and nothing else."

"Ew," Amanda shivered.

"But there weren't any," Mouse piped up and smiled at Amanda. "In fact it was really tidy in here. Then I found this box in the corner. It was full of stuff!"

"What kind of stuff?" Rebekah asked curiously.

"Stuff like this," Jaden said as he handed her a can of peanuts.

"Tasty," Rebekah said with a grin and opened the can. A brightly colored tube sprung out at her, bopping her right in the nose. "Ugh," she sighed, as she realized it had been a trick.

"And this," Max said as he pulled out the flower that Mouse had squirted her with.

"And this," Mouse smiled proudly as he held up a book. The title read:

Magic and Mischief: A Guide to Magical Practical Jokes

"Look," Mouse said as he flipped through the pages. "It's filled with all these little notes. Someone else was using this tree house before and this book. I think it was left here for other kids to find. Some of the tricks need more than one person, so I decided to see if anyone would be interested in starting a club."

"But you didn't tell me?" Rebekah asked with a frown.

"Well, you didn't seem interested," Mouse pointed out. "And since you kind of hurt my feelings, I thought I would make the club by myself. But, the truth is, I can't have any kind of club without you being part of it Rebekah! So what do you think? Do you think you could learn to like magic?"

Rebekah thought about this for a moment. She was certainly curious.

"If it means getting to hang out with all of you, of course I can," Rebekah said with a smile.

But she whipped out her notebook. She started making notes inside. Who built the tree house? Who left the book? Mouse had his very own secret magic club, but Rebekah had a brand new mystery to solve!

Rebekah – Girl Detective #12

The Missing Ice Cream

PJ Ryan

Rebekah - Girl Detective #12
The Missing Ice Cream

Chapter 1

As soon as Rebekah opened her eyes she was very excited. She had spent the whole night dreaming of Fudge Swirl, Cherry Garcia and Mint Chocolate Chip, all her favorite flavors of ice cream. Actually, there wasn't a flavor of ice cream that she didn't like. She would even settle for vanilla, if that was her only choice.

Rebekah hadn't been dreaming of ice cream because she went to bed early. She was dreaming of ice cream because today was the day she had been waiting for all spring. As soon as it was the official first day of summer, Mr. Sprool opened up the Ice Cream Shoppe and revealed to the whole town the brand new flavor he had created.

The flavor would only be around for the summer and Rebekah made it her job to be the very first one to taste it every year. So, as soon as the sun was up, her eyes were open and she was jumping out of bed.

She knew that Mouse would be doing the same thing. Each year they had a race to get to the Ice Cream Shoppe first. It was open all year long, but it was during the summer that they always highlighted a brand new ice cream flavor. Rebekah dressed quickly and put on her favorite ice cream cone t-shirt. Then she pulled on her shoes and raced into the kitchen. Her mother, who already knew what day it was, stood there with a banana and a glass of orange juice.

"No ice cream before breakfast Rebekah," her mother said firmly.

"But Mom," Rebekah started to complain. When her mother narrowed her eyes, Rebekah nodded quickly. "Okay, looks great, thanks!" she took the banana and the orange juice. She peeled the banana quickly, tossed the skin into the compost pile, and then scarfed it down. She followed it up with big swallows of her orange juice.

"Ugh, Rebekah you're going to make yourself sick," her mother shook her head with dismay.

"I can't help it," Rebekah giggled. "I can't wait to see what the new flavor is."

"Maybe it'll be orange banana," her mother teased with a smile.

"Nope, that was two years ago!" Rebekah reminded her.

"Oh that's right," her mother laughed. "Just be careful going into town, okay?"

"I will," Rebekah promised her. As she left the house she was glad she had something in her belly, because she was so excited that it was flipping and flopping.

Chapter 2

As Rebekah hurried down the sidewalk, she heard footsteps behind her. She knew whose they were before she even turned around.

"Mouse!" she said with a raised eyebrow.

"Rebekah," he replied with his hands on his hips.

"I guess no one wins this time," she laughed. "Why don't we just walk together?"

"Sounds good," Mouse nodded and they began to walk together toward the Ice Cream Shoppe. Their small town didn't have very much traffic, but they were still careful. When they reached the Ice Cream Shoppe, Rebekah saw Mr. Sprool flipping over the sign that hung in the glass door from closed to open.

"Hurry Mouse, before anyone else notices!" Rebekah said and began to run down the sidewalk. Mouse caught up with her just as she swung the door open. When Rebekah glanced over her shoulder at him, she noticed a small boy sitting at the corner of the shop. He had his head down and looked as if he might be taking a nap. Rebekah thought it was a little strange but she was too excited about the ice cream to pay too much attention.

"Hi Mr. Sprool!" Rebekah announced happily as she walked right up to the counter. It was high and silver, always cold to the touch. It came right to her shoulder, so she had to stand on her toes to peer over it and see the assortment of ice cream assembled in the cooler beneath. "I'm so excited to try the new flavor. What is it this year?" she asked, her eyes shining. "I do hope it has something to do with cherries and chocolate," she grinned.

Mouse nodded eagerly as he pushed his pet mouse gently back down in his front pocket. Mr. Sprool was not fond of Mouse bringing his pets into his store. "Or maybe something with peanut butter?" he asked hopefully.

"Hi Rebekah, hi Mouse," Mr. Sprool said quietly as he wiped a cloth along the other side of the counter. "I'm sorry but I'm afraid there's no new flavor this year."

"What?" Rebekah stared at him in absolute shock. "But that's not possible. You put out a new flavor every summer. Today's the day. What happened?"

He sighed and pushed his glasses up along his nose as he peered at Rebekah. He was an older man, in his eighties, and had owned the Ice Cream Shoppe for many years. He knew the parents of all the kids in the neighborhood from when they were kids themselves.

"I know you're disappointed Rebekah," he said with a slow shake of his head. "But there's nothing I can do about it. I whipped up the new flavor last night. I stuck it in the freezer and locked up. When I got here this morning to put it out, it was gone."

"Gone?" Rebekah repeated in a whisper.

"Stolen I suppose," he sighed heavily again. "It makes me so sad. Who would steal ice cream? I know I could make another new flavor, but until I find out who took the first, I'm not going to. I can't afford to waste supplies, and I had made this flavor very special," he frowned. "I guess I'm just a little upset about it."

"Of course you are," Rebekah shook her head slowly. "It is terrible that someone would steal the ice cream."

"Really terrible," Mouse agreed as he hung his head. It was very disappointing to wait all year for something, and then find out it wasn't going to happen.

"Would you like one of the old flavors?" Mr. Sprool suggested kindly. "I'm having a special on vanilla."

"Vanilla?" Rebekah sighed and shook her head. After having so many delicious flavors of ice cream she could barely think about plain old vanilla. "No thanks Mr. Sprool. In fact, I don't want any ice cream. I'm going to save my money because I am going to have a serving of your new flavor when I figure out who took it!" she said with determination.

"Now Rebekah," Mr. Sprool warned her with a steady gaze. "Someone broke in here and stole the ice cream. That someone is a criminal. You need to be very careful when you are dealing with a criminal."

"Oh I will be," Rebekah said with confidence. "By this time tomorrow Mr. Sprool, you will have your ice cream back. Do you mind if I look in the back room where the ice cream was stored?" she asked hopefully.

"Alright, but don't disturb the sprinkles," he said with a half-smile. "If anyone can solve this mystery, I'm sure it's you, Rebekah."

Chapter 3

She smiled proudly and began walking behind the counter. Mouse started to follow her but Mr. Sprool stopped him.

"Not so fast young man," he said with a gleam in his eye. "Don't think I didn't see that you have one of your rodents in your pocket. You'll have to take that thing out of my store. For all I know it could have been animals that got into the freezer."

"But it wasn't my mouse," Mouse said with a frown.

"Maybe not," Mr. Sprool said patiently. "But mice of any kind don't belong near ice cream. Okay?"

Mouse nodded sullenly. "Yes sir," he said and waved to Rebekah. "I'll take him home and meet you back here in a little bit."

"Okay Mouse," Rebekah smiled at him. "Don't worry, I'll have this solved in no time!"

Rebekah opened the door to the back room and paid close attention to everything she saw. She had never been there before. There were lots of bowls and mixers. Large boxes of sprinkles and other toppings lined the shelves. There was also one tall freezer. This was where Mr. Sprool said the ice cream had been. When she tugged on the handle of the freezer, it was very hard to open, which meant it had been closed tight.

"Not much chance an animal could have gotten this open," she said thoughtfully as she peered inside of the freezer. The shelves were coated with a layer of frost and ice. She could see where someone had scraped across the frost.

"Hmm," she said as she looked closely at a shape that was pushed into the frost. She whipped out her notebook and drew the shape on paper. It was a diamond shape. Then she closed the freezer and looked at the floor. She could see that there was some dirt on the floor. Mr. Sprool always kept his store very clean, so she had to guess that the dirt came from the thief. As she looked closely at the dirt she saw that it was arranged into neat little lines. Like the grooves on the bottom of a shoe. She looked at the bottom of her shoe. The grooves didn't match the pattern.

"Mr. Sprool," she called out. "Could you come here for a moment," she asked.

"Sure," he stepped into the backroom.

"Can I see your shoe?" she asked.

"My shoe?" he frowned but nodded and lifted his foot into the air. He swung his arms to keep his balance as Rebekah investigated the pattern on his shoe.

"Hm, doesn't look the same," she said as she abruptly let go of his foot. Mr. Sprool steadied himself and then peered at the dirt Rebekah was looking at on the floor.

"Well that's odd," he said quietly.

"I know," Rebekah tapped her pen lightly against her chin. "Mr. Sprool, I'm getting closer to the truth."

"Good," Mr. Sprool laughed a little. "I'll leave you to it."

Chapter 4

As he opened the door to step out of the back room, Rebekah noticed the back door swung open slightly. Her eyes widened because the door had been closed and locked a moment before. She walked over to it and looked at it very closely. When she tried to turn the knob, it wouldn't budge, but the door did swing inward very easily.

"Oh no," she whispered. The door was locked alright, but it had never been closed all the way. She crouched down and looked in the groove of the door. What she found was a large pebble that had been wedged into the door frame.

"So Mr. Sprool thought everything was locked up tight last night, but it wasn't," she said with a small smile. "This is how the thief got in!"

She was sure she was getting closer to the criminal, but the question still remained. Who had committed the unspeakable crime of stealing the newest ice cream flavor?

She pushed the door open and peered into the alley behind the store. It was empty aside from a big green dumpster. She didn't see anything strange, but she did notice a trail of dirt from the recent rainstorm. She crouched down to look at it closely. It was ordinary dirt with small pebbles mixed in.

As she reached the end of the trail she noticed that there were was a shoe print in the dirt. A shoe print with the same grooves as the pattern that she had seen inside the store.

"The thief definitely came this way," she said in a whisper. As she stepped outside of the alley and on to the sidewalk, she looked in both directions. There weren't too many people on the sidewalk. But she did notice a man waiting at the bus stop. She recognized him as one of the men who worked in the grocery store.

"Mr. Green?" she asked as she walked up to him.

"Yes," he smiled at her. "Hi Rebekah, how are you doing today?"

"Not so great," she frowned. "The Ice Cream Shoppe had its newest flavor of ice cream stolen."

"Oh no," he frowned. "That's terrible."

"I know," Rebekah agreed. "I was wondering if you'd seen anyone walking in and out of that alley," she pointed at the alley behind the store.

"Uh, well," he rubbed his chin for a moment as he thought about it. "Come to think of it, I did notice someone there yesterday. He was a small man, very short. He was standing at the end of the alley for a little while and then I saw him looking in the window of the ice cream shop. Then he disappeared down the alley."

"Could you tell me anything else about how he looked?" Rebekah asked as she noted in her notebook that the suspect was short.

"I didn't see his face," Mr. Green shook his head. "Then the bus came, so I had to go. I never saw him come out of the alley."

"Hm," Rebekah said as she heard the rumbling of the bus approaching. "Thanks Mr. Green."

"No problem Rebekah, I hope you solve your mystery!"

Chapter 5

Rebekah decided to walk down the sidewalk and around behind the stores that lined it. As she walked, she thought about the clues she had found so far. She knew that the person who had stolen the ice cream was short, that they had sneaked into the back of the shop through the alley and that they had something on their hands or wrist that had the shape of a diamond. She couldn't even begin to think of what that might be.

As she reached the end of the stores she looked up at the bright lights shining over the last store in the row. It was a dollar store that sold lots of novelty toys and items for very cheap prices. She peered inside the window out of curiosity. She saw they had some new magnetic travel games as well as some new race cars on the shelf. Then she noticed that there was a new display of jewelry. Rebekah knew she was on the job, but she wanted to take a quick peek. As she stepped into the store the woman behind the counter was looking through a magazine.

"Oh wow, a customer!" she said with a happy smile. "First one of the day!"

"Hi," Rebekah smiled at the woman. She didn't know her name, but she was always very friendly. "I just wanted to look at the new jewelry."

"Oh yes, it's been very popular," the woman said as she pointed to the display. "But it's not just jewelry, there are some watches in there too. I've already sold two of them and just got the products yesterday!"

"Wow," Rebekah looked at the watches and smiled. They were very unique. Each watch face had a different shape. One was a triangle, one was a square.

"Are these all the shapes they come in?" Rebekah asked curiously.

"No, they're just the ones I have left," the woman said. "I was just about to place an order for some more of the circle and diamond shaped watches. Those are the two I already sold."

"A diamond shape?" Rebekah asked with surprise. She pulled out her notebook and flipped it open. "Does it look something like this?" she asked, her eyes wide.

"Yes actually," the woman nodded. "Just about the same."

"Wow," Rebekah cleared her throat and began taking notes in her notebook. "Do you remember who bought this watch?" she asked.

"Yes," she nodded a little. "I remember because it was a young boy. He thought about his purchase for a long time. He had one dollar and kept rolling it up and unrolling it, as if he wasn't sure if he should spend it."

"Hm," Rebekah jotted down that a young boy had bought the watch. "Did he have his mother or father with him?" Rebekah asked.

"Actually no," the woman shook her head. "I've seen him in here a few times. He is always by himself. He doesn't usually buy much, only one toy, or sometimes he only looks."

"Do you have any idea what his name might be, or where he might live?" Rebekah asked with her eyebrows raised.

"Well I did watch him walk away the first time he was here. I was a little worried about a young boy being by himself, so I poked my head out to see if his parents were waiting for him outside."

"Were they?" Rebekah made another note on her pad.

"No, so I watched the boy walk down the hill. He went into the apartment building at the end of the street," the woman explained. "Are you looking for him for some reason?"

"Well, I'm investigating some stolen ice cream," Rebekah explained.

"What?" the woman said with surprise. "Who would steal ice cream?"

"That's what I'm trying to find out," Rebekah said with a determined frown. "Thanks for all of your help!"

"You're welcome," the woman smiled.

Chapter 6

Rebekah hurried out of the shop. She ran all the way to the end of the street. The apartments were very nice, with a playground and a pool. Rebekah loved to spend time with her friends who lived there because there was always somewhere new to explore or someone new to meet.

As she headed into the apartment complex she wondered how she would figure out which apartment this boy lived in. She still couldn't believe that a young boy would be behind the missing ice cream, but she had to follow the clues.

Just then she noticed footprints on the walkway toward the apartments. They were just like the footprints she had seen in the alley. She followed them all the way to one of the apartment buildings. They stopped at the stairs.

She climbed the stairs slowly, keeping her eyes peeled for any sign of a young boy. When she reached the second story she noticed that there was a different kind of trail. A trail of drips and drops of pinkish purple ice cream. She began to follow the drips until she reached one of the apartments.

Sitting in front of the apartment, with his back to Rebekah was a young boy. He had a container on the floor in front of him and a spoon in his hand. A hand with a diamond watch on its wrist.

This had to be the thief. All the clues were there. The dirty shoes, the ice cream container, the diamond watch. It made her sad to think it could be true, but the ice cream thief was a young boy. Rebekah folded her arms across her stomach and narrowed her eyes. She stared hard at the young boy who was devouring every last bite of the delicious new ice cream flavor.

"Just what do you think you're doing Mister?" She asked sharply as she walked up behind him. The young boy froze knowing that he was caught. His ice cream spoon hung in midair with a big dollop of the tastiest looking ice cream that Rebekah had ever seen.

"Put down the spoon and turn around," Rebekah said sternly. The young boy slowly lowered the spoon but before he laid it all the way down the ice cream on it began to melt and drip on to the floor beside him. There was nothing more terrible than seeing ice cream being wasted especially the brand new flavor.

"Oh just eat it," Rebekah sighed with frustration. "Hurry before it hits the floor," she insisted. The boy gulped down the ice cream that was on the spoon. Then he turned guiltily to look at her. It was the boy she had seen sitting outside the Ice Cream Shoppe earlier in the day. His hair was now very mussed and his lips and cheeks were covered with streaks of sticky ice cream.

"So it was you," Rebekah said coolly as she studied him. "Of all the people I suspected, I never thought it would be another kid. Sure, the grown-ups did, but me, never. Because I knew that all kids hold ice cream sacred, and no one would ever hog it all for themselves," she clucked her tongue at the young boy.

Chapter 7

"Most kids," the boy said with sadness in his eyes. "Would get a chance to taste it."

"What do you mean?" Rebekah asked him as she stepped closer to him.

"I mean, every year I watch all of the other kids in town get to taste the new flavor of ice cream," he sighed as he shook his head. "Everyone but me."

"Why not you?" Rebekah asked with confusion.

"I don't have any money to buy ice cream," he frowned and kicked the empty bucket of ice cream away from him. "This year, I saved all year. I was going to make sure I got a taste of the ice cream. But when I went into the dollar store and saw the watches, I knew I really needed a watch instead.

I'm always getting home late and my mother gets upset because she worries about me. But I am always losing track of time. So I bought the watch," he frowned. "But then I was really sad because I wasn't going to get any ice cream. So yes, I stole the ice cream, and yes, I ate every last bite. I never would have had the chance to taste it if I didn't."

Rebekah was stunned by his words. She had never met anyone who didn't have enough money to buy just one serving of ice cream.

"I'm sorry," she said as she shook her head. "But all you had to do was ask."

"You mean beg?" he shot back. "No way," he crossed his arms stiffly.

"Asking isn't the same as begging silly," Rebekah frowned and picked up the empty bucket of ice cream. "But stealing is wrong no matter how you look at it."

The boy nodded his head a little and stared at the empty bucket. "I know. I just wanted to try it so badly. I was watching through the window when he made it. I saw him add in all of the ingredients and I knew it was going to be the best flavor ever.

When he left for the night, a rock got stuck in the door and it didn't close all the way. He didn't notice I guess. I was just going to go in and have a look. I wanted to see what it was like. But once I was inside, I thought how nice it would be to have my very own bucket of ice cream."

"Well you're going to have to tell Mr. Sprool the truth," Rebekah insisted and pointed down the street toward the Ice Cream Shoppe.

"Alright, alright," he hung his head as he stood up.

"What's your name anyway?" Rebekah asked as they walked toward the Ice Cream Shoppe.

"Marcus," he said with a frown.

"Well Marcus just tell Mr. Sprool the truth and tell him you're sorry. Hopefully you won't get into too much trouble." She wasn't sure about that. Marcus had stolen an entire bucket of ice cream after all.

Chapter 8

When they reached the Ice Cream Shoppe, Mr. Sprool was just about to close up for the day. He saw Rebekah and the young boy so he opened the store back up.

"Hi Rebekah," he said with a smile. "Who's your friend?"

Marcus shifted from one foot to the other. He was a little scared.

"Hi Mr. Sprool," he said sadly. "I'm sorry, but I took a bucket of ice cream from your store."

"You did?" Mr. Sprool asked with surprise. He looked closely at the young boy. "Why would you do something so terrible?"

"I just wanted to try some," Marcus frowned. "I never get to try the new flavor."

Mr. Sprool scratched his head and looked sternly at the boy. "Well now no one will get to try it, because I lost my recipe for the new flavor. If you had just asked me, I would have let you try it."

"That's what I said," Rebekah pointed out.

"I'm really sorry," Marcus stared at the ground. "I didn't think it would cause that much trouble."

"Stealing always has consequences young man," Mr. Sprool said with a wag of his finger. "I hope this is the last time you do it."

"It will be," Marcus promised and looked up at Mr. Sprool again. "I think maybe I could help, if you would let me."

"Help how?" Mr. Sprool asked curiously.

"I watched through the window when you made the new flavor and saw everything you put in it. Maybe I could help you make a new batch," he said hopefully.

"You mean I might get to taste the new flavor after all?" Rebekah asked cheerfully.

"Okay," Mr. Sprool nodded. "Let's give it a shot."

Chapter 9

While Mr. Sprool and Marcus were working on the new flavor, Rebekah ran down the street and back into her neighborhood. She ran all the way to Mouse's house. Her legs were burning she was running so fast. Breathlessly she pounded on his front door.

"Rebekah?" he asked with confusion as he opened the door. "What is it? What's going on?"

"We just might get to taste the new flavor after all!" she said happily. "Hurry up and bring Neopolitan, you know how much he likes the cheesecake flavor. We can let him eat it outside."

"Okay," Mouse ran up the stairs to grab his pet and like a bolt of lightning he was back down the stairs. "Oh I can't wait to taste that new ice cream," he nearly squealed as he and Rebekah began running back toward the Ice Cream Shoppe.

"I found the ice cream thief!" she announced between gasps for air as they ran. "Now he and Mr. Sprool are making a new batch!"

They both skidded to a stop at the corner of the road and looked to make sure no cars were coming in either direction.

"What? How did that happen?" Mouse asked with confusion.

"Try to keep up Mouse," she sighed and then explained who the thief was, and why he had stolen the ice cream and how he had offered to help Mr. Sprool make more. Once they were sure it was safe, they hurried across the street.

"I never would have thought that a kid would steal the ice cream," Mouse said with surprise. "But at least you solved the mystery!"

Chapter 10

As Rebekah flung the door of the ice cream shop open Marcus and Mr. Sprool were just stepping out into the main area of the store.

"Well?" Rebekah asked. She was out of breath and her cheeks were red from running so fast.

"We did it!" Mr. Sprool said with a broad smile. "Ready to taste?" he grinned eagerly at the three children.

"Yes we are!" Mouse said happily as he whipped out his special spoon. It was a spoon that he reserved only for tasting the newest flavor on the first day of summer. Mr. Sprool set out three cups of ice cream on the metal counter.

"Thank you," Rebekah said as she picked up her cup and laid down her dollar.

"Thank you," Mouse said as he picked up his cup and laid down his dollar.

Marcus stood perfectly still staring at the last cup of ice cream. "I don't have any money," he said with a frown.

"That's okay Marcus," Mr. Sprool said and handed him the cup. "From now on, when I introduce a new flavor, everyone gets one free cup. No one should have to go without a cup of ice cream in the summer!"

"Thanks!" Marcus said with a smile and picked up the cup.

"Are you sure you can eat more?" Rebekah laughed as she quirked a brow at him.

"Once you taste it, you'll understand," Marcus said with a confident nod. He rubbed his stomach as if it was the most delicious thing he had ever tasted.

"Let's do it!" Mouse said as he slid his spoon into the ice cream. It was a strange pinkish purple color, a color of ice cream that Rebekah had never seen before. It had little brown flecks inside of it also. She thought she spotted something blue and squishy mixed in. It smelled very sweet, with a hint of chocolate. She took a small bite of the ice cream and let it melt on her tongue.

"Oh yummy," she sighed happily. "I taste raspberry, brownie and blueberry!"

"That's right!" Mr. Sprool said with a laugh. "You get it right every year Rebekah. "It is Raspberry Blueberry Brownie Bonanza!"

"I think it's delicious," Rebekah said as she took another bite.

"Me too," Marcus said proudly. "I'm glad I had the chance to make it."

Mouse couldn't say a word. His mouth was too full.

"I'm really glad that from now on everyone will have a chance to taste the new flavor," Rebekah added as she finished her ice cream.

"And from now on I'll just ask, instead of taking what I want," Marcus said with a shy smile.

Rebekah – Girl Detective #13

The
Ghost Snowman

PJ Ryan

Rebekah - Girl Detective #13
The Ghost Snowman

Chapter 1

Rebekah was very excited as she threw the last few things she needed to pack into her suitcase. It was already filled with extra sweaters, thick socks and a few scarves.

She was getting ready to leave on her annual ski trip with her family. But it wasn't just her parents that were going this year. Her cousin RJ, who was a few years older, was going along on the trip too.

She was so excited to see him, not just because he was her cousin, but because he had taught her everything she knew about being a girl detective!

RJ was a detective too and he solved mysteries in the middle of the great big city where he lived. Rebekah and RJ didn't get to see each other too often during the school year, so this ski trip was a very special treat.

Rebekah couldn't wait to tell him about all of the mysteries she had solved in her little town, where she was known as the best detective around.

When they picked up RJ in the city, he was excited too.

"Hi Rebekah!" he said happily as he climbed into the car beside her. "I see you're ready for the slopes," he laughed as he tugged at the bright pink earmuffs she was wearing.

"We're going to have to stay warm," Rebekah said with a grin. "Here, I got some for you too," she laughed. "They'll match your hat."

RJ always wore a detective hat. He had them in many different colors. As a seasoned kid detective, RJ was always on the look-out for mysteries, just like Rebekah was.

"Do you think that we'll find a mystery at the ski lodge?" Rebekah asked with a grin.

"I don't know," RJ replied with a shrug. "But if we do, I'm sure we'll be able to solve it!"

The drive to get to the ski lodge was pretty long. They had to drive along curved roads that got higher and higher as they drove. Rebekah and RJ didn't even notice the distance, because they were talking the whole time.

RJ told her about Joey, his friend, who he solved mysteries with. Rebekah told him about the mysteries she had solved at school. Then they both talked about Mouse's Secret Club, which they both belonged to.

Mouse, Rebekah's best friend, started the club. It was all about pranks.

By the time they were close to the ski lodge, RJ and Rebekah were laughing loudly in the back seat of the car. Rebekah's mother looked at them through the rear view mirror and grinned.

"We're not even there yet and they're already having a great time," she smiled happily.

"I can't wait to get on the slopes," Rebekah's father said. "We're supposed to get some snow while we're up there too kids," he called back over his shoulder. "So you'll get to build some snowmen."

"We're too old for building snowmen," Rebekah said with a sigh.

"No one is ever too old for building snowmen," Rebekah's mother said and laughed.

Chapter 2

When they arrived at the ski lodge, the sun was shining brightly. It made the snow sparkle. There was nothing that Rebekah liked more than the sight of the sun shining on the snow. There was still plenty of time for them to get out on to the slopes and Rebekah couldn't wait.

"Guys go ahead and get settled in, put your stuff away, then we have you set up to meet with an instructor so you can get skiing right away!" Rebekah's Dad said as he handed them each their suitcases.

"Dad we don't need a ski instructor," Rebekah frowned impatiently. "We already know how to ski."

"It's important to get a good reminder," her father said sternly. "If you want to ski, you have to go to the lesson. Understand?" he looked from Rebekah to RJ and back to Rebekah again.

"Yes Dad," Rebekah said with a sigh. They hurried to put their things away in the three bedroom cabin Rebekah's parents had rented for the weekend. There was plenty of room, and the fireplace in the living room kept the whole cabin toasty.

They bundled up in their coats and ski pants and hurried out to the bunny slope. That was where their instructor was waiting for them.

Rebekah thought he was a little strange because he was wearing a very fuzzy tall snow hat with big ears shaped like dog ears hanging off the side.

"Hi, I'm Matt, I'll be your ski instructor," he said cheerfully as he looked from Rebekah to RJ.

"We don't really need much instruction," Rebekah explained. "We've been skiing before." She wanted to get out on the slopes as soon as possible.

"Well it's always good to brush up on safety rules," Matt said firmly, although he was still smiling brightly. "So let's do our best to pay attention and follow the rules!" When he clapped his hands, the floppy ears on his hat shook back and forth.

Rebekah shot a funny look at RJ. RJ shot a funny look back at Rebekah. Then they both looked back at Matt.

Chapter 3

"Okay so there are three big rules of ski slope safety," Matt said cheerfully, his ears still flapping. "First, the whistles," he said as he held up two bright yellow whistles on necklaces. "It's easy to get lost on the slopes, especially if it's snowing. So you two need to make sure that you wear these at all times," he said firmly and handed them each one of the whistles.

"Thanks," Rebekah said and put on the necklace. RJ tried to put on his but it got stuck on his hat. He tugged harder and it finally went down over the hat.

"Thanks," he said quickly. "Now can we start skiing?"

"Wait a minute there little fellow," Matt said with a laugh and held up his gloved hands in the air.

"Little fellow?" RJ whispered to Rebekah with a frown. Rebekah tried not to laugh.

"There's a few more rules we need to talk about," Matt said as he paced back and forth in front of them.

"Now must of the time that you're on the slopes you're going to be on skis. But, if you happen to be walking on the slopes instead of skiing, please be very careful. The slopes are very slippery. One misstep and you could find yourself rolling all the way down to the bottom!" he shook his head at that.

"That sounds like fun," Rebekah said with a smile.

"No," Matt shook his head again. "Not fun. Dangerous little lady," he said and pointed his finger right at her. Rebekah's eyes widened. When Matt turned around, she looked over at RJ.

"Little lady?!" she rolled her eyes. RJ tried not to laugh.

"Now the last rule is the most important rule," Matt said sternly as he turned back. "These slopes are big. There are lots of trees around here. It's very easy to get lost. That's why you must always have a buddy when you ski. Always," he added as he looked at the two of them. "You should ski together and stay together at all times," he said sternly. "Understand?"

RJ and Rebekah nodded. They were familiar with all of the safety rules already so it wasn't hard for them to remember them again.

"Oh and there's one last thing," Matt said as he turned back to the two who were trying not to laugh over their instructor's comments. "Never, ever," he looked into Rebekah's eyes and then into RJ's eyes. "And I mean, ever, go outside after dark," he said in a very serious tone accompanied by a grim frown.

"What?" RJ asked skeptically. "Why?" he studied Matt.

"Oh you haven't heard?" Matt asked in a serious whisper. He wiggled his eyebrows a little.

"Heard what?" Rebekah asked with a raised eyebrow.

"About the ghost snowman," Matt said, still whispering. "That doesn't surprise me. Most of the staff that work here don't like to talk about it. But I wouldn't want you two to run into him by mistake."

"A ghost snowman?" RJ laughed out loud at that. "That's not possible. It doesn't even make sense."

"Believe what you want," Matt shrugged as he looked at RJ. "But if you're not careful, he might catch you."

"Catch us?" Rebekah shuddered a little. "Why would a ghost snowman want to catch us?"

"Okay, I guess I'll have to tell you the whole story," Matt said with a frown. "You see long ago, before this place was a ski lodge, there was a ghost that lived here. A ghost snowman," he added.

"Because that makes sense," RJ rolled his eyes. Rebekah kicked him with her ski boot.

"Just listen," she whispered to him.

Chapter 4

"The story goes that he was once a lonely old man who got lost in the middle of a blizzard. He turned into a snowman and wandered the slopes. When the ski lodge was built, the ghost snowman got mad. He didn't like all the banging and all of the people that were disturbing his snow," Matt explained.

"So he decided he would start capturing people from the ski lodge. He figured that if enough people went missing the ski lodge would have to close," Matt shrugged as if it made perfect sense to him.

"But it's still open," Rebekah pointed out. She found the story to be interesting, but she didn't really believe it.

"Well after the first few people were found shivering in the cold, everyone was told not to go outside of the cabins or the ski lodge at night.

The snowman ghost can only capture people at night, because he never goes out during the day. You know, snowmen and sunshine don't get along," Matt explained. "So to this day we warn everyone that stays here not to go out at night."

Rebekah tilted her head to the side as she thought about the story. She was pretty certain that a ghost snowman would want to avoid the sun if possible. Still, it was hard to believe.

RJ sighed and looked right at Matt. "Can we ski now?"

"Sure you can," Matt said with a shrug. "Just remember, don't go out at night!" Matt said in an eerie voice.

"We'll remember," Rebekah said, but her eyes were gleaming with excitement. As they got their skis on she whispered to RJ. "Sounds like a mystery to me!"

"Ghosts aren't a mystery," RJ shook his head as he snapped on his skis. "They don't exist."

Chapter 5

RJ and Rebekah decided to race down the ski slopes. Rebekah had a little more experience skiing, but RJ was a little bigger and heavier than Rebekah. So the race was pretty close.

When they reached the bottom of the hill, it didn't matter who won. They went right back up the hill to race again.

They had a lot of fun, but the whole time Rebekah's mind was on the snowman ghost.

Rebekah's mother was waiting with some hot cocoa. One with marshmallows for Rebekah, and one with cinnamon for RJ.

As RJ and Rebekah sipped their hot cocoa and warmed up in front of the fire they chatted about how much fun they had skiing.

"But can you believe that ski instructor?" RJ laughed. "Who ever heard of a ghost snowman?"

"Well, if he told us about it, then I bet other people believe it too," Rebekah grinned with a sparkle in her eyes. "What could it hurt to investigate?"

"Rebekah you're not really thinking there's a ghost snowman, are you?" RJ asked with a disapproving frown.

"Maybe not," Rebekah shrugged. "But it sounds like there might be some people that do believe there's a ghost snowman. So why shouldn't we look into it? We're here!"

"Good point," RJ laughed. "I guess we could check it out. He did say that the ghost snowman only comes out at night, so we'll have to go after dark."

"I say we take a quick nap and then sneak out after it gets dark," Rebekah said with a nod.

"It's going to be cold," RJ reminded her.

"Well that's what we have these lovely ear muffs for," Rebekah giggled.

"Another good point," RJ grinned and took a big gulp of his cocoa.

"Isn't that hot?" Rebekah asked with wide eyes.

"Yes, yes it is," RJ squeaked out. His cheeks were very red. After they finished their cocoa they went to their rooms to see if they could get a little sleep before heading out to investigate the mystery of the ghost snowman.

Chapter 6

When Rebekah lay down on her bed, she had a hard time falling asleep at first. She was excited to investigate with RJ, which was something she didn't get to do all that often.

She also was curious about the ghost snowman. Like RJ she didn't really believe in ghosts, but she was sure there had to be a story behind the ghost story. Maybe it was some kind of rare animal that no one had discovered before.

If she and RJ were able to capture it, they might be on the news! Maybe it was a yeti, a strange creature said to wander very snowy areas. Or maybe it was just another ghost story.

As she sorted through all of these ideas, she finally fell asleep.

While Rebekah slept, she dreamed of being out on the slopes all by herself. She was in the middle of a snowstorm. Everything was white everywhere she looked. Not only was it white, it was very very cold. The wind was blowing loudly and snow was swirling all around her.

"Rebekah!" she heard a voice call out from the swirling snow. "Rebekah!"

"Where are you?" Rebekah shouted back. She tried to see through the snow, but it kept blowing in her eyes. She was so very cold.

She suddenly realized she was wearing a bathing suit and flip flops. No wonder she was so cold! She was still wondering why she had chosen to dress for summer in the middle of winter, when she heard the voice again.

"Rebekah!" the voice called out. Rebekah was sure it was the ghost snowman calling to her. She had to find him! As she ran through the snow, she kept hearing her name called again and again.

"Rebekah!" the ghost snowman sounded annoyed that she hadn't found him yet. "Rebekah!" now he sounded a lot like RJ. Rebekah opened her eyes and looked right up into RJ's face.

"Sheesh, you are a deep sleeper," he said with a shake of his head. "I've been trying to wake you up for five minutes."

"Sorry," Rebekah said sleepily as she checked to make sure she wasn't actually in her swimsuit.

"It's time to go," he said in a whisper. "Your Mom and Dad are asleep and I've got the flashlights."

"Okay," Rebekah nodded and rubbed her eyes for a minute. "We need to make sure we bundle up."

Once they had on few sweaters, thick jackets and ski pants, they were ready to sneak out.

"I'm not sure I'll fit through the door," Rebekah giggled quietly as she was so bundled up that she could barely cross her arms.

"Shh," RJ reminded her. "We don't want to get caught before we even get out the door."

Rebekah nodded.

Chapter 7

Once they were outside, the cold hit them hard. Rebekah wished she had worn a ski mask to keep her face warm. She pulled down her hat and adjusted her ear muffs. RJ fixed his detective's hat and pressed his earmuffs hard against his ears.

"Stay close to me," he said sternly. RJ was only a little older than Rebekah, but he did like to act like he was in charge. Rebekah didn't mind, she was just excited to be solving another mystery with him.

As they walked out across the snow toward the ski slopes, Rebekah was amazed by how clear and bright the sky was. There were a lot of stars to see. She was glad they hadn't missed out on seeing them. RJ and Rebekah shined their flashlights in front of them to make sure that they wouldn't trip on anything.

"Why do you think people think it is a ghost snowman?" Rebekah asked with a frown. "It's kind of an odd thing to think of as a ghost."

"Look," RJ pointed his flashlight toward the trees. "Do you see that?" he asked in a whisper.

Rebekah pointed her flashlight in the same direction. She saw what looked like the outline of a figure. A very round figure.

"It's the ghost!" Rebekah said with surprise. "We found that fast!" she laughed.

"It looks like a ghost," RJ agreed as he walked bravely toward it. "But really it's just a snowman," he said as they reached it. "See?" he pointed to the carrot nose sticking out of the face of the snowman.

"People probably spot these at night and think they are ghosts, when they're really just snowmen left over from people making them during the day," he shook his head with a smile. "Ghost snowman mystery solved!"

"Well that wasn't much of a mystery," Rebekah frowned with disappointment.

"Did you really think there would be a ghost to find?" RJ asked. He put his flashlight under his chin so that his face glowed. "Watch out Rebekah! I'm a ghost! I'm going to get you!" he ooohed like a ghost.

Rebekah rolled her eyes and picked up some snow in her gloved hands. She mashed it into a snowball and threw it at RJ. RJ gasped and was scooping up some snow to throw one back at her, when Rebekah froze.

Chapter 8

"Shh, listen," Rebekah said as she grabbed RJ's arm. RJ stopped and listened closely. "Do you hear that?" Rebekah asked. They both heard crunching.

"It sounds like footsteps," RJ whispered back and glanced over his shoulder. "I can't see anyone."

"Maybe it's the ghost snowman!" Rebekah gasped and grabbed RJ's arm tighter.

"Rebekah," RJ sighed and narrowed his eyes. "Ghosts don't have feet. How could they make the sounds of footsteps?"

"Maybe this one does," Rebekah said with a frown. "What else could it be?"

"I don't know," RJ frowned. "But let's take a look."

He and Rebekah walked toward the sound of the footsteps. The closer they got to the sound, the more nervous Rebekah became. She didn't normally believe in ghosts, but the way Matt had talked about the ghost snowman made her wonder.

Suddenly the crunching stopped. RJ shined his flashlight around the snow covered ground.

"Look," RJ said in a hushed voice as he shined the flashlight on one spot.

"What is it?" Rebekah asked as she looked more closely. "Footprints!" she gasped. There were several of them in the snow. "They must belong to the ghost snowman."

"Rebekah-" RJ began to say.

"RJ hush," Rebekah insisted. "Let's follow the footprints, maybe we'll find the ghost, or whatever made the footprints that's not a ghost," she rolled her eyes. RJ nodded and they began to follow the footprints. They didn't hear the crunching anymore. But suddenly they heard another strange sound. It was a howling sound.

"Oh that sounds ghostly," Rebekah said with a shiver.

"I think you mean ghastly," RJ corrected her.

"No, I mean ghostly," Rebekah said as the howl came again.

"I don't think it's a ghost," RJ said. "But it does sound pretty eerie." Rebekah nodded in agreement. They continued to follow the footsteps for a little ways before they heard the howling again, only louder this time. It was so loud that it made Rebekah jump. She shined her flashlight in the direction of the howling.

"There it is again," she murmured. "That ghost is noisy."

"It can't be a ghost," RJ insisted with a stomp of his foot.

"Well let's go see what it is," Rebekah suggested bravely. "The footprints have stopped anyway," Rebekah pointed out as she shined her flashlight on the ground. "This must be where the ghost stopped walking and started floating."

"Or it could be where someone put on their skis and started skiing," RJ suggested as he pointed his flashlight at some ski tracks not far from the footprints.

"Maybe," Rebekah tilted her head from side to side as she considered it.

The next howl seemed to scream right over their heads. It was enough to get their attention again.

Rebekah ducked and looked up at the sky. "Whatever that is, I think we better find out where it's coming from, before it finds us."

"Good idea," RJ nodded.

Chapter 9

They began walking in the direction of the sound of the howling. As they walked toward the howling, all the leaves in the trees around them began shaking. They were rustling very loudly. It was a little strange. Rebekah pointed her flashlight up into the branches of the tree.

"What do you think is going on up there?" she asked with a frown.

"Probably just the wind," RJ shrugged and then shivered. "It's pretty cold when the wind blows!"

"I know, I wish we had worn ski masks," Rebekah shivered too and tightened the collar of her jacket around her neck. As Rebekah was speaking, they both saw a figure not far off. It was hard to tell just how far it was from them because it was so dark.

"Uh, do you think that's another snowman?" Rebekah asked in a whisper.

"Not this far from the lodge," RJ whispered back. As they were watching, the figure began to move toward them. They heard a loud shrill whistle.

"Ah!" Rebekah hid behind RJ at the strange sound.

"Even though I don't believe in ghosts," RJ said as calmly as he could. "I do think this might be a good time to run!"

Rebekah agreed with him, and they both began to run as fast as they could. The beams from their flashlights were bobbing up and down across the snow. It made the howling sound even spookier.

Finally, they had to slow down and catch their breath. Rebekah leaned on a nearby tree and peeked around it to see if the ghost, or whatever it was, was still behind them. She could hear the crunching, but she didn't see anything. What she also didn't see was the ski lodge.

"Uh, RJ?" Rebekah said in a whisper.

"What?" he gasped out as he was still trying to catch his breath.

"Do you know which way we're supposed to go to get back to the lodge?" she asked nervously.

"We just walk toward it," RJ said with a shrug. Then he looked in the direction Rebekah was looking. He only saw empty sky, trees and lots of snow. "Uh oh," he murmured. "Do you think we're lost?"

"We can't be lost," Rebekah said firmly. "Hey look," she pointed the flashlight toward the snow. "We can just follow our footprints back to the lodge."

"Good idea Rebekah," RJ said with a proud smile. "I never would have thought of that."

Chapter 10

As they followed their footsteps, they didn't hear the howling anymore. The trees weren't rustling so loudly either. It was actually pretty quiet. They had walked for a few minutes, when they suddenly heard the howling again.

"Eek!" Rebekah ducked behind the nearest tree. RJ ducked behind it too. The leaves in the tree were rustling quite loudly now, as if warning them to be careful.

"How are we ever going to get back to the ski lodge?" Rebekah whispered.

"Just wait, the howling stopped before, I'm sure it'll stop again," RJ whispered back. They waited for a few minutes as the howling got louder and louder. When the howling began to die down, they sighed with relief.

"Finally, let's get out of here," Rebekah said and started to step out from behind the tree. But before she could, they heard the crunching again. This time it was much louder. RJ pulled Rebekah back behind the tree.

"Stay back," he whispered. For once, RJ was a little scared.

"You know what, I'm not going to put up with this," Rebekah said with a frown and put her hands on her hips. "No ghost is going to scare me," she said sternly.

"What do you have in mind?" RJ asked as he looked at her curiously.

"I think we should scare the ghost first," Rebekah replied with a smile.

"Clever," RJ chuckled.

"Here get behind this tree," Rebekah instructed as she ducked down behind a large tree. RJ did the same and soon both of them were very well hidden by the thick trunk of the tree. They listened as the crunching drew closer to them. They could hear the howling still, though it didn't seem to be moving with the ghost.

"Wait for my signal," Rebekah whispered as they stayed crunched down.

"Okay, I think," RJ grinned as he peered around the side of the tree. He was still sure there was no such thing as ghosts, especially not a ghost snowman.

"Ready?" Rebekah whispered. "We're going to jump out and scare it when I say go, okay?"

"Okay," RJ nodded and got ready to jump out.

Chapter 11

"Go!" Rebekah shouted suddenly and jumped to her feet and out from behind the tree. RJ was right behind her. He roared and Rebekah shouted, "Boo!"

The figure before them let out a wild shriek. Then it slipped in the snow and started rolling down the ski slope. It wailed the whole time as it rolled down through the snow.

"Look at it go!" Rebekah gasped. "I can't believe we really scared a ghost!"

"I can't believe there really was a ghost," RJ said with wide eyes. "Hurry up, maybe we can catch it," he said.

He started running carefully down the slope. Rebekah followed after him, being very careful not to slip. When they reached the bottom of the slope they found what looked just like a snowman in a pile on the ground.

"Ugh," the snowman groaned. Rebekah and RJ stepped back a little. The snowman started to sit up. It dusted itself off and started to stand up.

"Uh oh," Rebekah whispered to RJ. "I don't think snowmen should be able to stand up and move around like that! Maybe we should run!"

"No!" the ghost snowman said sharply and started stumbling toward them. "No running! You two stay right there!" he grumbled and continued to dust himself off.

Chapter 12

As more and more of the snow was brushed off of his bulky jacket and ski pants, Rebekah and RJ began to realize that he wasn't a snowman at all. In fact, it wasn't a ghost either. It was Matt, their ski instructor!

"Matt!" Rebekah gasped and looked over at RJ who was just as surprised to see Matt.

"We didn't know it was you!" RJ frowned as Matt pulled off his ski mask and shook the snow off of it.

"Well I hope not," Matt growled. "Because I'm sure if you knew it was me, you wouldn't have shouted and made me roll all the way down that slope!" he said gruffly. He had his hands on his hips and didn't look too happy about being scared down the ski slope.

"What are you doing out here?" Rebekah asked with surprise.

"What am I doing out here?" Matt demanded. "What are you doing out here? I saw you two wandering around and I was worried that you would get lost, so I tried to catch up with you."

"We were looking for the ghost snowman," RJ explained with a sigh. "We didn't know it was you."

"You know kids, that story was meant to keep you from wandering around the ski slopes at night. Not to inspire you to wander around the ski slopes at night!" he shook his head as he pulled his ski mask back on. "What kind of kids would go hunting for a ghost instead of being scared of one?" he demanded.

"Well uh, we're not just kids," Rebekah explained with a grin. "We're detectives."

"The best detectives," RJ added. "We just wanted to solve the mystery."

"Well, you've solved it," Matt sighed. "There are no ghost snowmen. I just wanted to keep you safe. I guess I didn't do a very good job."

"Sure you did," Rebekah said with a smile. "RJ and I used the buddy system the whole time. We walked carefully on the slopes. We even made sure we brought our whistles," she showed him the whistle that was hanging around her neck.

"Well I guess the only one who wasn't safe was me," Matt laughed. "When I saw how windy and cold it was and heard all the howling of the wind through the mountains, I just didn't want you two to be out here alone. I even used my whistle to get your attention. But I'll admit, when you jumped out like that, it sure spooked me. That was one long roll down the hill," he added with a chuckle and a groan.

"It looked like fun," Rebekah said as they began walking back toward the ski lodge. "Was it fun?"

"I wouldn't recommend it," Matt laughed and shook his head. He led them back to the ski lodge. Rebekah was glad to get inside and get warm.

Even though it had been a little scary solving the mystery of the ghost snowman, she was glad that she had the chance to be a detective with RJ once again.

Rebekah - Girl Detective #14

Monkey Business

Chapter 1

Field trips were by far Rebekah's favorite part of school. It was a chance to be outside of the school with her friends and they always went to interesting places.

They were going to the zoo for their field trip and Rebekah was pretty excited. Her mother had given her a new camera to use on the trip because she wanted to see lots of pictures of the animals.

Mouse was excited too, mostly because they had a special exhibit of Malagasy Jumping Rats. Rebekah was a little unnerved at the idea of jumping rats, but she was excited because her best friend Mouse was excited.

At the top of Rebekah's list to see was a young monkey that had been born only a few weeks earlier. The zoo had made a big deal of welcoming the baby, and even held a contest to see who could name it.

It was a lot of fun to take part in the contest and Rebekah was eager to see what the monkey had been named.

On the bus ride to the zoo she and Mouse talked about the different animals they would see. Rebekah also played with her new camera. She was snapping a picture of Mouse when his pet mouse poked its head up out of his pocket.

"Oh no you brought a mouse?" Rebekah hissed so the teachers wouldn't hear.

"He didn't want to miss it!" Mouse said with a frown. "Don't worry it's just Gabe, he likes to be very quiet and hide in my pocket."

"I hope so," Rebekah frowned. "Because if he gets loose in the zoo it's going to be very hard to find him."

"I know," Mouse nodded.

Chapter 2

When they reached the zoo the teachers paired them up with buddies. Rebekah chose Mouse, of course, and they were off to see the animals.

As they walked through the zoo Rebekah was looking over a map that she had been handed at the entrance. She wanted to get to the monkey section as soon as she could, because she knew it would be very crowded.

Mouse was looking at a map too and he started walking in the opposite direction toward the rodent area.

"Stay together kids!" Mrs. Duncan called out from behind them. Her voice was very loud because she had brought along a bull horn. Rebekah and Mouse looked up at the same time to see that they were walking very far apart.

"Oops," Rebekah laughed as she walked over to Mouse. "I'm sorry I wanted to see the monkeys."

"Oh," Mouse frowned with disappointment. "I was hoping to see the Malagasy Jumping Rats first."

Rebekah frowned too. She really wanted to see the monkeys, but she knew that Mouse was excited about the rats.

"Okay we'll go see the rats first," Rebekah nodded. "But then you have to let me take a picture of you with the monkeys!"

"Alright, fine," Mouse grinned. As they hurried toward the rodent section of the zoo, Rebekah nearly bumped into a boy who was running in the opposite direction.

"Excuse me," Rebekah said as she stepped aside so that they wouldn't slam into each other.

"Sorry," he mumbled and hurried off. Rebekah noticed that he was carrying a bunch of bananas. It was a strange snack to bring to the zoo, but she only shrugged and followed after mouse.

While Mouse oohed and ahhed over the jumping rats, Rebekah snapped pictures of them and other animals nearby. She even got a picture of one of the teachers running from the lion cages.

It wasn't until Rebekah turned back around that she realized that Mouse was leaning very far over the side of the rat enclosure.

"Mouse!" Rebekah squeaked and ran over to him. She reached out just in time and caught Gabe before he could fall in.

"Oops," Mouse took Gabe from her and tucked him back into his pocket. "Sorry Rebekah," he grinned sheepishly.

"Just keep him in there," Rebekah said firmly. "Can we go see the monkeys now?" she asked hopefully.

"Sure," Mouse nodded. "Would you mind taking a picture of me with the rats?" he asked.

"No problem," Rebekah agreed. She took a few steps back and waited for one of the rats to jump. Then she took a picture of Mouse, with a rat over his shoulder and a mouse poking its head up out of his pocket. She had to admit it looked pretty funny.

She decided to take one more picture, but before she could the same boy who she had almost bumped into earlier, walked right in front of the camera. He had his jacket bundled up in his arms.

"Sorry, sorry," he said as he hurried through the picture. Rebekah was so surprised that she accidentally took the picture.

"One more," Rebekah sighed. Mouse was getting tired of smiling but he managed to hold it long enough for Rebekah to get another good picture. As they walked over to the monkeys, Rebekah was still a little annoyed.

"That boy was so rude," she said with a frown. "He didn't have to walk right in front of the camera. He could have walked around. Do you know him?" she asked.

"I think his name is Lucas," Mouse said with a shrug. "He's not in any of my classes, but I remember him from an assembly about animal rights. I went to it because of my mice, poor little guys are always being used as lab rats."

"I've never seen him before," Rebekah frowned. "He must not be in my classes either."

"Oh well, don't let it ruin our day," Mouse said with a smile. "Up next, a picture of Mouse with the monkeys!"

Rebekah laughed and followed after him to the monkey section of the zoo.

Chapter 3

Just as Rebekah had expected, the monkey section of the zoo was packed. It seemed like everybody wanted to see the littlest monkey at the zoo. As she and Mouse tried to get closer, Rebekah realized, the crowd was buzzing. But it wasn't because of the cute little monkey. It was because the monkey was missing.

"Where is he?" one of the teachers whispered to another.

"Could he have gotten loose?" one of the kids wondered. Rebekah noticed one of the zoo staff members standing beside the cage. He looked very sad. Rebekah and Mouse slipped over to him.

"Is the little monkey really missing?" Rebekah asked with a frown.

"Yes," the zookeeper sighed. "I just checked on him fifteen minutes ago and he was snuggled up to his Mom. Now he's gone!"

Rebekah frowned as she thought of the poor little monkey without its mother. She looked at all the kids and teachers that were bunched around the cages.

"Don't worry," she said with a smile. "We can all help you look!"

The zookeeper thought about it a moment and then nodded. "That's actually a very good idea," he said. The crowd was so noisy that it was hard to get their attention. So Rebekah found the teacher with the bull horn.

"Can you announce to everyone that the zookeeper has something to say?" she asked politely.

"I can do better than that," Mrs. Duncan said. "I can give him the bull horn."

She handed over the bull horn to the zookeeper and he turned it on.

"Excuse me!" he said, and looked a little startled by how loud his voice was. "Excuse me," he tried again, and soon all of the people in the crowd were quieting down. "I'd like to ask for your help," the zookeeper said calmly. "Our little monkey is missing. I don't know how he got out, but we need to find him.

Since there are so many of you here, I thought we could all search together." All of the people in the crowd shouted that they would help.

"We've never had an animal escape before and I want you to know that this monkey is not aggressive. He won't hurt you, but he might be very scared. So if you spot him, please don't pick him up just let one of the zoo staff know that you've found him," the zookeeper then began splitting up everyone in the crowd into smaller groups, each with a teacher to lead them.

Rebekah and Mouse were assigned to Mrs. Duncan who was beside herself with concern.

"Poor little monkey. We've got to find him. What if he wanders into one of tiger cages?" she sighed.

"Maybe we should check in the most dangerous spots first," Rebekah suggested. She really wanted to go off to search by herself, but she knew that she had to stay with the teacher. Rebekah was a very good detective and a missing monkey was a mystery she knew that she could solve. She just had to think it through.

Chapter 4

"Mrs. Duncan, what if the monkey didn't escape?" she asked thoughtfully. "What if someone took him?"

"Oh Rebekah I don't think that's what happened," Mrs. Duncan shook her head. "Who would steal a monkey?"

Rebekah frowned, but she didn't think she was wrong. It was the cage itself that made her think someone took the monkey.

The zookeeper said he had just checked on the monkey a few minutes before it went missing. Maybe he had left the door to the cage open? But when Rebekah had looked at the cage, it was all locked up.

She did notice from the picture of the monkey on the display that it was very tiny. Some of the bars on the monkey cage were a bit wider than the others. Maybe he had slipped out. But if he was snuggled up with his mother why would he want to leave the cage?

Rebekah waited until everyone had cleared out from in front of the cage.

"Mrs. Duncan, I need to use the bathroom," Rebekah said quickly.

"Alright Rebekah. Mouse you walk with her, you are her buddy," Mrs. Duncan said sternly. "And both of you meet us by the tiger cage, okay?"

"Yes Mrs. Duncan," Rebekah nodded. Mouse glanced over at Rebekah as Mrs. Duncan walked away.

"You don't really have to use the bathroom, do you?" he asked as he looked at her.

"No," Rebekah admitted. "I wanted to take a closer look at the cage."

"Do you really think someone took the monkey?" Mouse asked with surprise.

"It just doesn't make sense to me that he would escape," Rebekah said with a frown. "Don't you think someone would have seen him if he slipped through the bars?"

"You're right," Mouse nodded. "Everyone was there to see the little monkey, I'm sure they would have said something if he was sneaking out."

"Look at his," Rebekah said as she pointed out the lock on the door of the cage. "It's locked up tight. There's no way it was left open. But no one would have been able to break in either."

"Maybe someone had the key?" Mouse suggested.

"Maybe," Rebekah frowned. She noticed the zookeeper talking with a police officer that had been called to help aid in the search. "We should ask the zookeeper who has keys to the cages."

Chapter 5

They waited for the zookeeper to finish talking to the police officer, and then walked over to him.

"Excuse me sir, can I ask you a question?" Rebekah asked.

"Sure," he nodded, but he was very upset.

"Who has keys to the monkey cages?" Rebekah asked.

"Only me," the zookeeper sighed. "I'm the only one with the key. I know I locked the door," he added.

"And you're sure the monkey was there when you checked?" Rebekah asked with a frown.

"Yes I'm sure," the zookeeper nodded. "I noticed that his bowl was empty so I was going to get him some food. He was sleeping, and I knew when he woke up he would be hungry. I just don't know how this could happen," he said with a shake of his head. "I'm always so careful," he sighed as he walked away. Rebekah found it hard to believe that the zookeeper would be careless. He seemed to take his job very seriously. She suspected something else must have happened. But if no one else had the key, how could anyone have gotten the monkey out?

Rebekah peered through the bars of the monkey cage.

"Look at that," Rebekah said as she pointed to something inside the cage.

"What is it?" Mouse asked as she looked where she pointed.

"It looks like a banana peel," Rebekah said with narrowed eyes.

"Well monkeys do like bananas," Mouse reminded her with a shrug.

"But the zookeeper said he had been going to get food for the little monkey," Rebekah explained. "He said the bowl was empty. That banana peel looks fresh. So where did it come from?" she asked.

"That is odd," Mouse agreed. Rebekah decided to get a closer look at the peel. She couldn't get inside the cage, but she could zoom in with her camera. She did just that and snapped a picture. As she studied the picture on the back of her camera she nodded.

"It's definitely a banana peel and it's bright yellow so there's no way it's been sitting in there for very long," she said firmly. "No Mouse, I don't think this little monkey escaped. I think someone helped him out of the cage."

"But how?" Mouse asked. "There's a roof on the cage."

"Well these bars are further apart than the others," Rebekah pointed out as she measured the distance between the bars with her fingers. "That monkey is very little and he probably could squeeze through here."

"But remember, people were watching," Mouse said with a frown.

"Good point," Rebekah sighed and shook her head. "This is a tough one."

"Let's think it through," Mouse said. "If you think that someone stole the monkey, then you probably think someone gave him the banana."

"A banana!" Rebekah snapped her fingers. "Remember that boy? He had a whole bunch of bananas!"

"Oh that's right," Mouse nodded. "But that doesn't mean he's the one who gave the monkey the banana."

"No it doesn't," Rebekah agreed. "But there was something else odd too," she said quietly. "Remember when he walked through the picture of you with the rats?" she began flipping through the camera. "When I saw him with the bananas the first time, he was wearing his jacket. When he walked through the picture he was carrying it," Rebekah recalled.

"Well it did get a bit warmer out," Mouse pointed out.

Chapter 6

"Hm," Rebekah looked down at the picture she had accidentally snapped of the boy. She made it larger on the screen. As she did her eyes widened. "Uh Mouse," she showed him the picture. "That jacket has a tail!"

"Oh wow!" Mouse gasped as he saw the brown tail sticking out from the end of the jacket. "You're right Rebekah. Do you think he's really the one who stole the monkey?"

"Think about it," Rebekah said in a whisper. "The monkey woke up hungry and Lucas had bananas. He probably tossed the monkey one of the bananas. Then when the monkey wanted more, he took off his jacket. He could have laid it against the bars so that no one would see the monkey slipping through the bars to reach for another banana!"

"Wow," Mouse shook his head. "I wouldn't think a kid could do this," he frowned as he glanced over at the police officer who was interviewing some of the people who had been standing beside the monkey's cage. "Lucas isn't a bad kid Rebekah, but if he gets caught, he's going to be in big trouble."

"I know," Rebekah said with a frown as she glanced up at the officer too. "That's why we've got to find him before anyone else does."

Mouse glanced at his watch. "If we don't get back to Mrs. Duncan, we're going to be the ones in big trouble."

"Good point," Rebekah frowned. "Let's see if we can find out which group Lucas is supposed to be in," she suggested.

As they walked off to rejoin Mrs. Duncan and the rest of their group Rebekah saw all of the kids, teachers and other zoo visitors searching for the monkey. She knew that she should tell the zookeeper about the picture she had, but she didn't want to get Lucas into too much trouble.

If they could just find him, maybe they could convince him to give the monkey back. Rebekah glanced over her shoulder at the monkey cage and saw the little monkey's mother looking sadly through the bars.

"We have to find Lucas," she said firmly.

Chapter 7

"Oh good, there you two are," Mrs. Duncan said with a sigh. "What took you so long?"

"We thought we saw the monkey in a tree," Rebekah explained with a shrug. "Sorry."

"It's okay, it's just that they have shut all of the exits of the zoo and I wanted to make sure you were safe," Mrs. Duncan explained.

"So no one is able to leave the zoo?" Rebekah asked with surprise.

"No, they're afraid the little monkey might escape through one of the exits, so they have it all locked up!" she glanced around at the other animal cages around them. "I just hope they find him soon, this wasn't exactly what we had planned for our field trip."

"Well we better start looking," Rebekah said. "Maybe we should check the elephant enclosure," she suggested. "That's very open and the monkey could hop right in."

"Good idea," Mrs. Duncan nodded and started to lead the kids toward the elephant enclosure.

"Very clever," Mouse whispered to her. "The elephant enclosure is all the way at the back of the zoo so we'll have to walk past all of the other groups to get to it."

"Exactly," Rebekah nodded. "So keep your eyes peeled."

"I will," Mouse promised. "Lucas couldn't have gotten too far, and that monkey isn't going to stay hidden in his jacket for too long."

As they walked, several of the zoo staff members were checking all of the animal cages. They checked everything from the giraffes, to the bird sanctuary, to the crocodile cage. But they all came back out with a frown and no monkey.

Rebekah knew how badly the zookeeper felt for the baby monkey going missing. Everyone seemed to think it was his fault and only Rebekah, Mouse and Lucas knew that it wasn't.

Chapter 8

"There!" Mouse pointed to a group that was gathered beside a glass enclosure filled with porcupines. "I think that's him," Mouse whispered to Rebekah.

Rebekah saw a boy standing at the back of the group. He had his jacket on, but he had it on backwards. It was odd to see, but no one else seemed to notice it.

"It is him," Rebekah hissed as she pointed to a brown tail that was sticking out of the bottom of Lucas' jacket.

"Hurry we have to get to him," Rebekah said as she and Mouse started to break away from their group.

"Where are you going?" Mrs. Duncan asked from right behind them. "I told you two to stay close."

Rebekah frowned as she turned to face Mrs. Duncan. "I'm sorry, we thought we saw something by the porcupines."

"Mr. Tuttle's group is looking over there," Mrs. Duncan said firmly. "Please we already have a missing monkey, I don't want to have a missing Mouse or a missing Rebekah!"

"Sorry Mrs. Duncan," Mouse said and shoved his hands in his pockets. When Mrs. Duncan walked back to the front of the group, Rebekah's eyes widened.

"That's it! A missing mouse!" she said as she looked at Mouse.

"Huh?" Mouse asked.

"You're going to have to distract everyone. Actually, Gabe is going to have to distract everyone," she said and pointed to the mouse hiding in his pocket.

"Oh but Rebekah like you said the zoo is so big and-" Mouse frowned.

"Don't worry," Rebekah promised him. "We'll make sure he's safe. I'll go on one side of the path, and you go on the other. Let Gabe run across and scare everyone, then I'll catch him."

"Alright," Mouse finally nodded.

Chapter 9

They hung back a few steps behind their group. Then Mouse let his pet free on one side of the path.

"Eek! Mouse!" Rebekah cried out as the little white blur bolted across the path.

"Mouse?" Mrs. Duncan asked, thinking that Rebekah was talking about her friend. Then she saw the white blur.

"Mouse!" she shrieked. Rebekah reached down to catch Gabe, but Gabe was scared of her. He was a very timid mouse and he ran in the other direction. He ran right into the elephant cage! All of the elephants started trumpeting and stomping when they saw the mouse in their enclosure.

Mouse gasped. "Gabe!" he cried out. Rebekah felt horrible. She had promised Mouse that his pet would be safe.

She spotted Lucas looking over at the commotion. All of the groups were gathering together to see what all of the shrieking was about. Rebekah knew that if she didn't catch Lucas now he might get away, but she had promised Mouse that Gabe wouldn't get lost.

She turned back in time to see the little white mouse bolt right out of the other side of the elephant cage.

"Come on Mouse!" she called out and they ran after Gabe. Mouse almost had him, when he slipped into the enclosure with the jumping rats. The rats started going wild, jumping everywhere.

"Oh no!" Mouse slapped his forehead. "We're never going to get him out of there," he groaned.

"Sure we will," Rebekah said sternly. She glanced in one direction, and then in the other. Everyone was busy looking for the monkey. No one was looking at the jumping rat cage.

She handed Mouse her bag and camera and then jumped right into the cage.

"Rebekah!" Mouse gasped and nearly dropped her camera. He accidentally took a picture of Rebekah surrounded by jumping rats.

"Do you see him?" Rebekah asked as the rats jumped all around her. She had to duck when one tried to land on her head.

Mouse looked down at the picture he had taken and spotted Gabe in the corner of the cage.

"In the corner!" he called to Rebekah. "Hurry before he gets away!"

Rebekah caught Gabe in her hands and carried him back to Mouse. Mouse tucked him safely into his pocket and then helped Rebekah out of the cage.

"Thank you so much Rebekah!" Mouse sighed with relief.

"I promised to keep him safe," Rebekah frowned. "Too bad we can't do the same for the little monkey. I bet Lucas is long gone by now."

Chapter 10

"That was very brave Rebekah," Lucas said from beside her.

"Lucas?" Rebekah gasped as she looked at him.

"I saw what you did," Lucas said as he hugged his jacket that was hiding the little monkey. "You must really love animals like I do."

"Well, it was Mouse's pet," Rebekah explained as she looked at the tail swishing at the bottom of his jacket. "Just like that little monkey is his mother's baby," she said softly.

"But he shouldn't be in a cage Rebekah," Lucas said sternly. "The animals should get to live free, in the wild where they belong."

"But Lucas, how is he going to survive without his mom to teach him how to?" Rebekah asked. She didn't want to make him angry and have him run off. "I know that you want to protect the little monkey, but so does the monkey's mom."

"I don't know," Lucas frowned. "I think he needs to be free. I can take care of him."

"Oh Lucas, you can't have a monkey as a pet," Mouse said with a shake of his head. "Monkeys need a lot of care. Maybe being in the zoo isn't the best place for him, but it's where his family is, and they will take very good care of him."

"How do you know?" Lucas asked.

"Look," Rebekah pointed to the zookeeper who was sitting on a bench with his head in his hands. "Look how upset he is that the monkey is missing. He really cares about the animals he takes care of."

"I guess you're right," Lucas frowned. "But what can I do now? If I tell the truth, I'm going to get in a lot of trouble."

"That's for sure," Mouse nodded as he noticed a few more police officers had entered the zoo.

"Well maybe we can put the monkey back instead," Rebekah suggested. "If you could sneak him out, we can sneak him back in!"

"But everyone is looking for him now," Mouse reminded Rebekah.

"We can do it," Rebekah promised. "Let's give it a try."

Chapter 11

Since the monkey cage had been searched so well when the little monkey first went missing, there weren't too many people around it. But Mrs. Duncan was looking for Rebekah and Mouse, so they had to be careful.

They walked behind the cages and hid behind trees as they crept toward the monkey cage. The little monkey was getting restless under Lucas' jacket. He kept whipping Lucas with his tail.

"Shh," Lucas pleaded with the monkey.

"It's okay, he just wants his mother," Rebekah said sadly. "Look, she's waiting for him," Rebekah said and pointed to the monkey cage. The little monkey's mother was standing class to the bars and seemed to be looking for the monkey.

"It's now or never," Lucas sighed. "I guess I didn't think this through."

"You wanted to protect him," Mouse shrugged. "I know what that's like. But now he needs to go back to his mother."

Lucas took a deep breath and began walking across the path to the monkey cage. Rebekah and Mouse followed close behind him. Just like Lucas had done before, he took off his jacket and used it to hide the monkey.

The little monkey held his breath and squeezed through the bars of the cage. His mother was waiting for him on the other side.

"Rebekah? Mouse?" Mrs. Duncan was calling as she walked toward the cage.

"Lucas, go back to your group," Rebekah said in a whisper. "That way no one will know you were here."

"Are you sure?" Lucas asked with a frown.

"You did the right thing," Mouse nodded. "Just blend in and ditch the rest of those bananas, huh?" Mouse pointed out the bananas that Lucas still had in his pocket.

"Okay," Lucas nodded. He tossed them into the monkey cage before running off to the group he was supposed to be with.

"Rebekah and Mouse," Mrs. Duncan said from right behind them. "You're both in big trouble. I told you to stay with the group!"

"We were," Rebekah said with wide eyes. "But then we saw this and had to look closer to make sure we were right!" Rebekah explained.

Chapter 12

"Saw what?" Mrs. Duncan asked as she looked where Rebekah was pointing. The little monkey was wrapped up in his mother's arms.

"Oh the monkey!" Mrs. Duncan cried out getting everyone's attention. "The monkey is back!"

The zookeeper came running back over. He couldn't believe his eyes.

"But I searched that cage myself!" he said. Once all of the cheering had died down, Rebekah pulled the zookeeper aside and spoke in a whisper to him.

"You might want to check the bars on the cage," she said. "That's one skinny monkey."

The zookeeper looked right at her. "I know that monkey was not in the cage," he said with a frown. "You and your friend had something to do with this, didn't you?"

Rebekah looked at him nervously. She wondered if he was going to be upset.

When she didn't answer, he just smiled. "Look I don't know how you did it, but I'm happy you did. In fact, I'm so happy, I want you to be the one to name the monkey. We haven't picked a winner yet."

"Really?" Rebekah asked with surprise.

"Sure, can you think of a good name for him?" he asked. Rebekah looked over at Mouse who had Gabe in his hand and was talking softly to him about the monkeys in the cage.

"Mouse!" she said with a laugh.

"Mouse?" the zookeeper raised an eyebrow. "A monkey named mouse is a little strange, but alright!"

Chapter 13

All the way home on the bus the kids talked about the newest little monkey at the zoo, a monkey named Mouse.

When Rebekah got home, her mother was very excited to see the pictures from the zoo.

"I didn't get too many," Rebekah frowned as she handed over the camera. She was tired from the exciting day, so she headed to her room for a rest. Rebekah's mother began looking through the pictures on the camera. Rebekah had just lay down on her bed when she hear her mother gasp.

"Rebekah!" she shouted. Rebekah sat bolt upright in bed, her eyes wide.

"Yes?" she asked as she ran out to the living room.

"Can you explain why you were inside a cage of jumping rats?" her mother asked as she tapped her foot and held out the camera.

Rebekah gulped as she looked at the picture of all the rats jumping around her.

"Uh, that's kind of a long story Mom," Rebekah said with a laugh.

"Good, we've got plenty of time," her mother said and sat down on the couch. She patted cushion beside her. "I want to hear all about it."

"Did you know I got to name a monkey after Mouse?" Rebekah asked as she tried to change the subject.

"Next time there's a field trip to the zoo, I'm going to chaperone," her mother shook her head as she looked through the rest of the pictures. "Does that boy have a tail?" she asked as she tilted the camera to the side.

"Well uh, that's a longer story," Rebekah laughed and shook her head. She was glad to have solved the mystery of the missing monkey, but she was a little worried about whether her mother might decide to do some detective work of her own.

Rebekah - Girl Detective #15

Science Magic

Chapter 1

One of Rebekah's favorite classes was science. Not just because of the subject, but because of the teacher. Rebekah had a few science teachers in the past that were pretty great. But by far her favorite was her current science teacher, Mr. Woods.

He was always thinking up new ways to teach them fun science concepts. Rebekah looked forward to his class because she saw science as just another mystery to solve.

One day Rebekah walked into Mr. Woods' class to see something very surprising. In the middle of his desk was a strange cylinder. In the middle of the cylinder a small square magnet was floating in midair!

"Wow!" Rebekah said as she looked at it closely. "How is that happening?" she wondered.

"Magic!" Mr. Woods said as he stepped up behind his desk.

"Oh Mr. Woods I don't believe in magic," Rebekah shook her head. As a detective, she had solved many mysteries. Some of them looked pretty magical at the start, but they always ended up being something much simpler than she expected.

"Well, this is science magic," Mr. Woods explained with a grin. "Look," he opened a small door on the plastic cylinder and poked his finger against the magnet. It moved, but it still floated. "See?" he said. "No strings."

'Wow," Rebekah said with wide eyes.

"Oh that old trick," Max laughed as he walked into class. Max was one of Rebekah's friends. His father was a scientist, so science was his favorite class.

"Don't tell Max!" Mr. Woods warned him. "I want Rebekah to figure it out."

"Oh she will," Max laughed. "Rebekah can figure anything out!"

Rebekah smiled at Max, then she looked back at the floating magnet. As the other students filed into the class, Rebekah continued to stare. No matter how much she thought about it, she couldn't figure out how the magnet could be floating in midair the way it was. It was really beginning to bug her.

Chapter 2

"Alright class, today we have a special assignment," Mr. Woods said as he sat on the edge of his desk. "This is what I call science magic," he said as he pointed to the cylinder. "Did you figure it out yet Rebekah?" he asked as he looked over at her.

"I think so," Rebekah said thoughtfully.

"Well, why don't you tell us how you think it's done?" he asked with a smile.

"It's a trick," she said.

"No it's not a trick," Mr. Woods said firmly. "A trick is an illusion. This isn't an illusion. This magnet is really floating."

"Well there must be some kind of trick," one of the other kids called out. "Is there a fan or something?"

"No, no, fan," Mr. Woods said. "But that's a good thought."

"Rebekah, what do you think?" he asked and looked back at Rebekah.

"Well I know that magnets can push each other apart," Rebekah said with a frown. "Does it have something to do with that?"

"Absolutely," Mr. Woods said with a smile. "We have some special, powerful magnets here. See this one on top is a ceramic magnet," he explained as he pointed to the magnet at the top of the cylinder. "This one on the bottom is a magnet as well. They are repelling each other. The magnet in the middle is caught in the middle of their little fight," he grinned. "That's the easiest way to explain it."

"That's pretty amazing," Rebekah said with wide eyes.

"Yes it is," Mr. Woods said with a nod. "Science is pretty amazing. Sometimes we forget that science is a study that is constantly changing and growing. People are always discovering something new about our world and the laws of nature and science."

"Like scientists," Rebekah pointed out.

"No, not just scientists," Mr. Woods corrected her. "Some of the greatest discoveries have been made by average people, who stumbled on to a great idea.

That's what our assignment today is about. I'm not going to give you a set of directions. I'm going to ask you to come up with an amazing new idea. Then I want you to make it work. No volcanoes, or potato electricity," he said firmly. "Something new that you think of yourself. It really doesn't matter if it works. I just want to see what ideas you can come up with."

Rebekah liked the assignment already. It was like a mystery that she could solve. What new idea could she think of?

"Oh what's the point?" Bethany, another girl in the class grumbled from her desk behind Max. "It's not like any of us have a chance with Max in our class."

"Hey," Max frowned as he glanced over his shoulder. "That's not very nice."

"But it's true," Bethany crossed her arms. "No one is going to think of a better project than you."

"Let's all do our best," Mr. Woods said as the bell rang. Max glared at Bethany. Bethany glared back at Max. Rebekah frowned. Bethany was very good at science too, but she was always competing with Max in class.

"I'm sure we'll all come up with something," she said, hoping to cool off the tension between her friends.

Chapter 3

After class Rebekah was still thinking about the project she would create. She was very excited about the idea. She met her friend Mouse in the hallway by her locker.

"Guess what? Mr. Woods has a great assignment!" Rebekah said happily.

"I've heard," Mouse said happily. "Did you see the magnet trick? We could use that in a prank!" he laughed. Rebekah nodded.

"I bet we could," she grinned. Mouse had his own secret club that thought up great pranks that they could pull on people.

"I'm trying to think of a great idea," Rebekah said with a frown. "But it's harder than I thought!"

"Don't worry, you'll think of something," Mouse promised her.

By the time school was over that day Rebekah still couldn't think of anything. Any idea she came up with had already been done. She wanted something different, something that would showcase her talents as a detective. As she was putting her books away at the end of the day, Max walked up to her locker.

"Hey do you have an idea yet?" Max asked with a grin.

"Not yet," Rebekah frowned. "Do you?"

"Oh yeah, I've got a great one!" Max smirked. "But it's a secret."

"A secret huh?" Rebekah smiled.

"No detective work Rebekah!" he warned her with a wag of his finger.

"No way," she promised. "I'm too busy thinking of my project, to figure out yours!"

"Well Mr. Woods said we have a week, so that will give you plenty of time," Max smiled. "Good luck!"

Chapter 4

Rebekah spent the whole week trying to come up with an idea. By the time Thursday night came around, she still didn't have a clue what to do. She was very disappointed. She decided to call Max to see if he could help her.

"Rebekah, I'm not telling you about my project," Max said as soon as he answered the phone.

"I was just hoping you might have an idea for me," Rebekah sighed. "I can't think of a single thing."

"Well you can always stick a carnation in a glass of water with food dye," he said with a laugh in his voice. "That's an easy project."

"Thanks a lot Max," she said with a sigh. She knew it was a simple project, but at least she would have something to turn in. "How is your project coming along?"

"It's great!" Max said enthusiastically. "I can't wait to show everyone tomorrow."

"Can't wait to see it," Rebekah said happily. She hung up the phone and went to look for her mother.

"Mom, do you know where we can buy a carnation and some food dye?" Rebekah asked just as her mother was sitting down to read her new book.

"Oh dear, do we need it now?" she asked.

"I need it by tomorrow morning," Rebekah cringed.

"Oh Rebekah," her mother shook her head.

"Sorry Mom," Rebekah smiled innocently.

When they reached the store, Rebekah hurried to pick out a flower. She spotted Bethany not far off. She had several bottles of paint, glue, and even some large Styrofoam balls in her arms.

"Hi Bethany," Rebekah said as she picked her flower. "Do you need some help?"

"No thanks," Bethany said with a frown. "No peeking at my project!"

"Okay, okay, sorry," Rebekah smiled. Bethany did not smile back. She walked right to the check-out lane. Rebekah was going to be glad when the assignment was over.

When she got home she put her flower in water with bright pink food coloring. Then she went to bed.

When she woke up the next day, her white carnation was bright pink.

"Well at least it worked," she shrugged. She stuck the carnation in a plastic zip-lock bag and tucked it into her bag. She was excited about seeing both Max and Bethany's projects.

Chapter 5

When she got to school she found Max standing beside his locker.

"Ready to turn in your project?" Rebekah asked from just behind him, causing him to jump.

"No peeking Rebekah!" Max growled and closed his locker.

"I wasn't peeking," Rebekah said as she rolled her eyes. "This project has turned you and Bethany into monsters!"

"Science monsters," Max wiggled his eyebrows.

"See you at class," Rebekah laughed. After her first class Rebekah stepped out into the hall. She was greeted by a loud scream.

"Someone stole my project!" Max frowned as he looked in his locker. "I put it in here this morning, and it's not here now!"

"Are you sure someone took it?" Rebekah asked. "Maybe you misplaced it?"

"I didn't," Max said firmly. "I put it right here to keep it safe until science class. Someone took it!"

He turned around and found Bethany standing not far from his locker. "Was it you?" he asked her with a glare.

"No!" Bethany gasped and shook her head. "It wasn't me."

"I know you were jealous about my project," Max argued with frustration. "Did you take it so that Mr. Woods would like your project best?"

"No, I didn't," Bethany said with tears in her eyes. "I didn't, I really didn't Max."

Rebekah frowned as she put an arm around Bethany's shoulders. "It's okay, don't get upset she said."

"She should be upset," Max huffed. "She took my project. I know she's the one who did it."

"But I didn't," Bethany argued and sniffled. "You have to believe me Rebekah."

Rebekah frowned. She and Max were good friends, but she had never known Bethany to steal anything. Sure she had been determined to create a better project than Max, but that didn't mean she would do something as terrible as stealing it. But if she didn't take Max's project, then who did?

"We'll see what Mr. Woods has to say about it," Max said firmly and started walking off toward the science classroom.

"Oh no, now Mr. Woods is going to think I'm a thief too," Bethany sighed. "You know I didn't do it, don't you Rebekah?" she asked hopefully.

"Sure I do," Rebekah said quietly. "Don't worry about Max, he's just upset. Mr. Woods won't believe him. Especially if I figure out what really happened to Max's project."

"Oh I hope you do," Bethany said and sniffled again. "I don't want Max to be angry with me."

Chapter 6

Rebekah found Max heading for the principal's office to report Bethany.

"Max wait," Rebekah said as she chased after him. Mouse caught up with them too, as he wondered what all the shouting was about. "Maybe it wasn't Bethany," Rebekah said. "Why don't you let me try to figure out what happened?"

"Alright," Max nodded. "If anyone can figure it out, it's you Rebekah," he sighed. "But I'm sure it was Bethany."

"Listen, in order for me to figure it out, you're going to have to tell me what your project looked like," Rebekah said.

"It was goo," Mouse admitted. "Bright green goo. That should be hard to hide."

"Okay, we're going to find it, aren't we Mouse?" she glanced over at Mouse who was petting the top of the head of a mouse in his top shirt pocket.

"Yes, we will," he said with a nod.

"We'll have to start with your locker," Rebekah said.

Max wrote down the combination for her. "I hope you can find it," he said with a frown as he walked off to his next class.

Rebekah and Mouse hurried to Max's locker. Rebekah unlocked it and opened it up. Inside it was pretty empty. But it had a strange smell. It wasn't a bad smell, like when Mouse left pieces of cheese for his mice in his locker for too long. It was a sharp smell, like lemon.

"Weird, Max doesn't smell like lemon," Rebekah said as she sniffed the locker.

"What does Max smell like?" Mouse laughed.

"I'm not sure, but it's not lemon," Rebekah giggled. Then she looked more closely at the door of the locker. She crouched down and looked at the bottom to see if it might have been pried open. It wasn't, but there was a bit of green goop on it.

"Hm," Rebekah said as she rubbed the goop between her fingers. "We have green goo," she said and looked up at Mouse with a grin.

"Gross," Mouse shivered a little.

"Well if no one broke into Max's locker, then someone must have had another way to get in," Rebekah said thoughtfully. "Or maybe," she looked at the small air vents on the front of the locker. "Maybe someone got that strong vacuum they used to vacuum up that overflow in the boys room. If they put the hose up to the air vent, maybe they vacuumed the goo right out!"

"Who would do that?" Mouse said with a frown.

"I don't know, but it's a place to start," Rebekah suggested. Just then the bell rang.

"Meet me near the janitor's closet when class is over," Rebekah said quickly.

Chapter 7

Her next class was with Bethany. She noticed that Bethany looked very sad as they read a story in English class. She had a big bag beside her desk. Rebekah thought it probably had her science project in it.

Rebekah looked closely, but she didn't see any green goo on the bag. As soon as class was over, Rebekah waited for Bethany to leave. Then she looked over her desk closely for any traces of goo.

She didn't find anything at all, but she did smell something familiar. It was a sharp scent. It smelled like lemon. Rebekah's eyes widened. She didn't think that Bethany had taken Max's project, but why did her desk smell like Max's locker?

She hoped she wasn't wrong about Bethany. When she met Mouse beside the janitor's closet he looked a little nervous.

"I was thinking about something Rebekah," he said as she opened the door to the janitor's closet. "When you said someone could have used the vacuum to suck the goo out of the locker, it reminded me of something else that is good at sucking."

"What?" Rebekah asked as she ducked inside the closet. She found the vacuum pretty fast because it was pretty big.

"Like a vampire!" Mouse said as he kept watch for her.

"That's ridiculous Mouse," Rebekah rolled her eyes. She picked up the hose attached to the vacuum. "Aha!" she said. "Look," she stuck her finger inside the opening of the hose and came out with her finger tip covered in green goo. "I was right!"

"That doesn't mean it wasn't a vampire," Mouse pointed out.

"It's not a vampire Mouse," Rebekah said firmly. "But now we have to figure out who used the vacuum."

"Well it wasn't the janitor," Mouse said. "Remember Mr. Hugh retired last week."

"Good point," Rebekah nodded. Mr. Hugh was the janitor at the school but the teachers had a party for him to celebrate his retirement. So there shouldn't have been a janitor to use the vacuum. "Whoever used this vacuum took Max's science project," she said with certainty. As she stood up she caught a whiff of that strong lemon scent again. She sniffed until she found where it was coming from.

"Look at this Mouse," Rebekah said as she showed him a bottle of lemon scented cleaner. "This is what I smelled in Max's locker. I also smelled it at Bethany's desk. Maybe she really did take his project. If she came in here for the vacuum, she might have spilled some on herself."

"Who's there?" A voice bellowed from the shadows in the back of the closet. "No kids should be in here! I'm warning you! It's very dangerous!"

Mouse and Rebekah looked at each other, and then ran out of the closet. They ran all the way to their next class.

"See, I told you it was a vampire!" Mouse said with a gasp. "Someone living in the shadows, someone dangerous," he added.

"It can't be," Rebekah rolled her eyes. "Meet me outside the cafeteria after lunch."

"I'll be there," Mouse promised. "Watch out for vampires!"

Chapter 8

During her next class Rebekah tried to think of different ideas. She was pretty sure it hadn't been Bethany, even though some of the evidence pointed to her. Whatever had yelled at them from the back of the janitor's closet, certainly hadn't been Bethany.

Once she had scratched Bethany off of her suspect list, she was back at square one for suspects.

She pulled out her notebook and stared down at a blank page of paper. Since she had no other good ideas, she scribbled: Green Goo Eating Vampire. She knew it was a silly idea, but at least it was an idea.

Then she thought about Max some more. Everyone knew Max was the best science student in the school. She was sure his project would have been the best in the class. Maybe someone wanted the project. Maybe someone like an evil scientist, or someone who worked for an evil science spy agency.

She arched an eyebrow and jotted down her idea. It made about as much sense as a goo eating vampire. She sighed as she realized neither idea was going to solve the mystery.

If she didn't figure out who had really taken Max's project, he might stay mad at Bethany. He might even turn her in to the principal. Rebekah hated to think of Bethany getting into trouble for something that she didn't do. She was determined to figure it out, and hopefully before science class.

At lunch time Rebekah was waiting for Mouse outside of the cafeteria. Most of the other kids were already out of the hallway. She was waiting in a small hallway that led to the bathrooms. It was the only place the lunch monitor wouldn't spot her. The hallway was pretty dark.

When she started hearing heavy footsteps walking toward her she was surprised. She glanced over her shoulder, but she didn't see anyone behind her. Then she heard the footsteps again. Rebekah looked over her shoulder again. She still didn't see anyone. But she did smell something. Lemon! Rebekah gasped and turned back just in time to find Mouse standing right in front of her.

"Are you okay?" Mouse asked when he saw her wide eyes.

"He's here," she whispered to him and pulled him behind the open girls' bathroom door. They both watched as a man with his head down trudged slowly past the bathroom. He had thick boots on. He reached down and wiped a paper towel over one of them. When he pulled the paper towel away, Rebekah had to cover her mouth to keep quiet. There was green goo on the paper towel!

He grumbled and tossed the towel into a trash can. Then he started trudging down the hall again.

"See, vampire," Mouse whispered. "What kind of person walks like that?"

Rebekah watched as the man seemed to be struggling to pull his feet off the floor with every step he took. It was rather odd.

"Well let's find out," Rebekah said sternly. "Come with me!" she said.

Chapter 9

They followed the man down the hall. When he opened the door to the janitor's closet, Rebekah and Mouse looked at each other.

"One, two, three!" Rebekah counted down. Then both Mouse and Rebekah shoved the man from behind. They were going to trap him in the closet. But when they tried to close the door, it was stuck. It wouldn't budge. They heard groaning from the back of the closet. Rebekah pulled out a penlight and shined it into the closet. She shined it right at the shadow of the man in the back of the closet.

"Who are you and what have you done with Max's goo?" Rebekah asked as she shined the flashlight right into the man's face.

"Hey, stop that!" he grumbled and pushed the flashlight away. "That hurts my eyes."

"See I told you he's a goo eating vampire," Mouse whispered beside Rebekah's ear.

"I'm not a vampire!" the man said and shook his head. He pushed his way out of the closet. "You kids are acting up. I'm going to tell the principal."

"Wait a minute, what kind of criminal tells the principal?" Rebekah asked with a frown.

"I'm not a criminal, I'm the janitor," the man said with a frown. "My name is Mr. Potter and it's my first day. Some first day," he added gruffly. "First I get sticky goo stuck to my shoes, then I have to clean all the desks in the English classroom because somebody sprayed silly string, and now I get shoved into a closet by a couple of kids," he shook his head.

"Oh," Rebekah's eyes widened as she realized the mistake they had made. "Sorry about the whole shoving you in the closet thing," Rebekah said with a sheepish smile.

"Why did you do it?" Mr. Potter asked with a glare. "Is it just because you kids like to pick on janitors?"

"No way!" Mouse shook his head.

"That's not it at all," Rebekah frowned. "Someone stole our friend Max's science project, and we thought it was you. We thought you might be a spy from some secret science agency," she explained calmly.

"Actually, I thought you were a goo eating vampire," Mouse pointed out.

"Some imaginations you kids have," Mr. Potter shook his head. "I didn't steal any science project. I'm not a spy for any science agency, and I'm no kind of vampire!"

"Sorry, but you did have some of Max's goo on your shoe," Rebekah pointed to the man's goo covered shoe.

"Oh that?" Mr. Potter shook his head. "Look, I wanted to make a good impression. I was walking down the hallway this morning, and I almost slipped and fell in a puddle of this green stuff," he sighed. "So I cleaned it up, but a few seconds later there was a new puddle!

That's when I realized it was leaking out of the bottom of one of the lockers. So I opened up the locker and cleaned it up," he explained. "There was some glass on the bottom of the locker too, so I cleaned that up too."

"Oh," Rebekah's eyes widened. "That must be what happened!"

Chapter 10

Just as she was about to tell Mouse her suspicion, the bell rang.

"Get to class kids, so you don't get in trouble," Mr. Potter said with a grave frown. "We'll just keep this little mishap between us."

"Thanks," Rebekah said with relief. She didn't want to have to deal with a trip to the principal when she had finally figured out the mystery! She waved to Mouse who hurried to his class while Rebekah headed for Mr. Woods' class. When she ducked inside Max was standing in front of Mr. Woods' desk with a frown.

"I don't have a project to turn in," Max said sadly.

"Well to be honest Max I'm very disappointed," Mr. Woods said with a shake of his head. "Out of all the kids in this class I expected you would at least turn in the assignment."

"I tried Mr. Woods, but someone stole it!" Max said and glowered over his shoulder at Bethany.

Bethany looked down and frowned. She pulled the big plastic garbage bag beside her closer to her desk.

"No max, no one stole it!" Rebekah said as she walked up behind Max. She was out of breath from practically running to class.

"What?" Max asked with surprise.

"Your green goo, was it in a glass container?" she asked.

"Yes, a glass beaker I brought from home," Max nodded.

"Well, I think that somehow the glass must have broken, and all the green goo was seeping out of the bottom of your locker. Mr. Potter the new janitor saw it and cleaned it all up. That's why you thought it was stolen!"

"Oh," Max said softly. "I was experimenting with combining some different chemicals to make super goo, maybe they caused the goo to expand so much they broke the glass."

"That would have been some interesting super goo," Mr. Woods said with a smile. "Alright Max, it's clear to me that you did do the assignment, so I will give you credit for it," Mr. Woods smiled.

"Thanks," Max said sadly. Then he turned around and walked over to Bethany. "I'm sorry I accused you Bethany."

"It's okay," Bethany said. "I'm sorry I acted so jealous. That super goo sounds like it would have been pretty great."

"Thanks," Max said, I guess I need to work on it a little more though.

"Maybe you should use plastic instead of glass," Bethany suggested. "Like a plastic bag, that way it can expand if the goo expands."

"What a great idea!" Max grinned. "Want to come over after school and try it out?"

"I would love to!" Bethany said happily. "Want to see my project?" she asked with a smile.

"Yes please," Max nodded.

Chapter 11

Bethany carried the bag up to the front desk. She opened it up and placed the objects on the desk. "Remember when someone mentioned a fan in class?" she said. "It gave me an idea. I wanted to create a project on the impact of different wind speeds on stationary objects," she explained. "So I created this."

When she put it together, it was a model of trees, small mountains and pools of water. "I thought if we could figure out the perfect speed to move each one, we might be able to figure out how to protect each one from harm if there's bad weather."

"Great idea!" Mr. Woods clapped his hands loudly. "Wow Bethany, I bet the meteorologist at the local news station would love to see this project. Do you mind if I tell him about it?"

"Not at all," Bethany blushed shyly.

"That really is a great project," Max said as he studied it closely. "You might be able to make a very important discovery because of this Bethany. I'm really impressed."

"You?" Bethany asked with surprise. "Really?"

"Yes really," Max laughed. "It's a whole lot better than some super green goo!"

"Green goo would be a lot more fun," Bethany pointed out.

"The important question is what happens when you combine a certain wind speed with some super green goo," Rebekah asked from behind other of them.

"Oh no!" Bethany laughed at the idea.

"You'd sure have a gooey situation," Max joked, making all three of them laugh.

"Alright kids, we need to get started with class," Mr. Woods said as he waved them to their desks. Rebekah walked slowly to her desk. She wasn't looking forward to sharing her project with the class.

Rebekah was walking to her desk when Mr. Woods called out to her. "Where's your project Rebekah?" he asked. Rebekah sighed. She picked up her book bag.

Rebekah pulled the carnation out of her book bag that she had colored with food dye.

"Not very creative, I know," she said with a frown as she laid it on Mr. Woods' desk.

"You know Rebekah, I think your project was the most creative of all," Mr. Woods said with a smile.

"A flower?" Rebekah asked with surprise.

"No not the flower, although that is fun to do," Mr. Woods grinned. "I'm talking about your mystery solving," Mr. Woods laughed. "How did you figure it out?" he asked.

"Well," Rebekah frowned. "I smelled lemon and I felt goo, and I knew there was no such thing as green goo eating vampires," she shrugged. Mr. Woods raised his eyebrows.

"Okay," he said with a slight shake of his head. "Well, that's what I mean. You used a lot of scientific techniques to figure out just what happened to Max's project. Without your senses you wouldn't have been able to figure it out.

Good job! No one else has demonstrated how science is used to solve mysteries, so I'd say that your project was very creative after all! Wouldn't you?" he asked.

"I guess so," Rebekah beamed proudly. She always knew that science was just another kind of mystery, and she was determined to solve it. She was just going to make sure she wasn't around when Bethany and Max did their wind and green goo experiment. That was one mystery she didn't have any desire to solve.

Rebekah - Girl Detective #16

Quiet On The Set!

PJ Ryan

Rebekah - Girl Detective #16

Quiet On The Set!

Chapter 1

Rebekah flipped through the pages of the magazine on her bed. She was looking for pictures of one person in particular. Danny Dakota.

Danny Dakota was a big star, at least to Rebekah he was. He played a detective on the hit television show, "Justice for Kids" and she thought he was the best actor in the world.

Danny was just a year older than she was and she was amazed that he could be on television. Not only was he on television, but he was going to star in a movie about his television show. She couldn't wait for the movie to be out so that she could see it in the theater.

When her phone began ringing, Rebekah didn't want to answer it. She wanted to read an article about Danny's movie. She finally answered it on the fifth ring.

"Hello?" she said.

"Hi Rebekah, it's RJ," her cousin RJ said into the phone.

"What's going on RJ?" Rebekah asked with a smile. She always loved to hear from her older cousin. He had taught her everything she knew about being a detective. While Rebekah lived in a small town, he lived in the big city and they had a great time talking about mysteries.

"Well I heard this rumor," RJ said. Rebekah could hear the excitement in his voice.

"Rumor about what?" she asked as she sat up and pressed the phone closer to her ear.

"About Danny Dakota and his new movie," RJ replied. "I know how much you like the show, and Danny, so I thought I should tell you what I heard."

"What? What did you hear?" Rebekah asked eagerly. She was holding the phone so tightly that her fingers were going numb.

"Hensely said he saw some camera men outside of the apartment building today while I was in school. The camera men were looking for a good place to film one of the scenes for the movie. So Hensely suggested they use the lobby!" RJ said excitedly.

"The lobby of your apartment building?" Rebekah asked with a gasp. RJ's parents were the managers of the apartment building they lived in.

"Yes!" RJ laughed. "I think they're going to be shooting here this weekend. Do you think your parents would let you come visit?"

"I'll ask right now!" Rebekah squealed and hung up the phone. She ran out into the living room where her parents were watching a television show. "Can I go to RJ's this weekend?" she asked hopefully.

"Sure if you like," her mother nodded. "As long as all of your homework is done," she added.

"It will be!" Rebekah promised. She was so excited that she called RJ back right away to let him know that she would be there. She knew that she might not get to see Danny Dakota, he might not even be in the scene, but it would still be amazing to see part of the movie being filmed.

Chapter 2

Of course no matter what Rebekah did, she couldn't leave out her best friend Mouse. She called him right away to see if he could come with her to RJ's too.

Mouse's mother agreed that they could spend the night on Saturday, but on Sunday they had to be home early because it was a school night.

Rebekah was very excited when her mother drove them both to RJ's apartment building. RJ was waiting for them with a wide grin.

"Guess what?" he said as soon as they got out of the car.

"What?" Rebekah asked after hugging her mother goodbye.

"They're really going to be here!" RJ said. "First thing in the morning!"

"Oh wow!" Rebekah clapped her hands. Mouse rolled his eyes a little. "Oh you know what we have to do?" Rebekah asked with a big smile.

"What?" both RJ and Mouse asked.

"Danny Dakota marathon!" she squealed and ran into the apartment building.

"Oh no," Mouse groaned.

"What exactly is a Danny Dakota marathon?" RJ asked with a raised eyebrow.

"It's when Rebekah pulls up all of the episodes on the computer and watches them. All of them," Mouse hung his head slightly. "We're going to need snacks."

"Yes we are," RJ laughed and shook his head. "I like the Danny Dakota show, but not that much."

"Don't worry, I brought my pet mouse Hollywood. We can teach him some tricks," Mouse said as he showed RJ the mouse in his pocket.

"Oh good, but don't let my Dad see him," RJ warned. "He's a little touchy about mice in the building."

"I won't," Mouse promised.

Chapter 3

That night while RJ and Mouse taught Hollywood to run through a maze made of books and shoes to get some cheese, Rebekah watched at least ten episodes of Danny Dakota on the computer.

Even though she already knew what happened in the episode, she was still impressed when Danny Dakota figured out the mystery.

RJ and Mouse fell asleep long before Rebekah did. When she finally turned off the computer, all she could think about was Danny Dakota and all of the mysteries he solved.

The next morning she was so excited she woke RJ and Mouse up early.

They met Hensely in the lobby. Hensely pointed out all of the equipment that the staff members were bringing in. Even though they were up early, the lobby had already been filled with props and decorations.

Rebekah admired the large cameras that were rolled into position to film the scene. The lobby of RJ's apartment building was completely transformed from a run of the mill lobby to what looked like a very dark and scary mansion. It made Rebekah excited for the upcoming movie.

"Do you see him Mouse?" she whispered to her friend who was trying to keep his pet mouse in his pocket.

"Not yet," he replied with a smile. Mouse knew how much Rebekah liked Danny Dakota. Mouse didn't really enjoy the show, he liked comedies better, but he would always watch it with Rebekah if she wanted to. He thought Danny was a good actor too, but he wondered what it would be like to be a kid and have to act like someone else all day.

"Look!" Rebekah pointed with excitement. "It's Dylan Banner, he plays Danny Dakota's uncle and arch nemesis in the movie," she sighed as she watched Dylan Banner stride across the lobby. She wasn't as big of a fan of him, but if he was there, maybe Danny Dakota would be too.

"Here guys," RJ said as he brought them over two bottles of water. "We can't get upstairs for a while, so the staff is handing out water. Did you see him yet?" he asked Rebekah with a grin.

"No, maybe he won't be here," Rebekah shrugged a little. "But this is still amazing!"

"It is pretty cool," RJ admitted. He pointed to a man in a big brown hat with a red scarf tied around his neck. "That's the director," he said. "He says when they will start filming."

"Oh boy!" Rebekah took a sip of her water. "I can't wait to see this in the movies and know that I was here when they filmed it."

"Well it is exciting, but sometimes scenes don't make it into the movie," RJ warned. "It would be so cool if this did though!"

Chapter 4

"Quiet on the set!" a very tall and very thin man shrieked from the opposite corner of the lobby. Rebekah, Mouse and RJ did their best to be very quiet.

"Action!" shouted the director. Dylan Banner began pacing back and forth. It was amazing to Rebekah how he went from being just a guy walking around, to looking very evil, as if he was about to do something terrible.

"He'll never stop me," Dylan Banner chuckled darkly as he paused in the middle of the lobby. "Once and for all, I've defeated Danny Dakota."

"Think again, uncle!" a voice cried out from the other side of the lobby. When Rebekah looked up she saw that a ladder and platform had been brought into the room. Standing on top of it with a rope in his hand, was none other than Danny Dakota. Rebekah's mouth dropped open. Mouse's hand clamped over her mouth before she could let out a squeal.

"Shh," RJ reminded her in a whisper. Rebekah nodded quickly and took a breath. Danny jumped off of the platform and swung right through the lobby. He landed right on top of Dylan Banner's shoulders.

"You'll never win," he growled and covered his uncle's eyes.

"Ah!" Dylan cried out and tugged at Danny's hands. He wandered around as if he couldn't keep his balance. Rebekah was worried that Danny might get hurt. Then she saw all of the cushions that had been laid out on the floor to protect him just in case they fell.

"Look at that," Mouse whispered as he saw one of the cushions inflate. He was leaning down to get a closer look when Hollywood slipped right out of his pocket.

"Oh no," Rebekah gasped when she saw the mouse escape.

"Shh!" a member of the movie staff hissed at her.

"Peek-a-boo uncle!" Danny cried out and lifted his hands off of his uncle's eyes. Rebekah had no idea what was supposed to happen in the movie, but she was sure that what did happen had nothing to do with the movie.

Chapter 5

"Mouse!" Dylan Banner shrieked. "There's a mouse!" he began running around in a circle with Danny still on his shoulders.

"Cut!" the director called out. Rebekah slapped her forehead and closed her eyes for a moment. Mouse was trying to sneak on to the set to get Hollywood before someone with a broom could. RJ grimaced.

"Oh dad's not going to like this," he muttered under his breath.

Dylan lost his balance with Danny still on his shoulders and went tumbling down on to one of the cushions. People were running in all directions, some from the mouse and some to the mouse.

There was chaos in the lobby and some of the props even fell over. Mouse finally retrieved Hollywood and hid behind Rebekah and RJ hoping that no one would figure out that it was his mouse that caused all the commotion.

"Keep him in your pocket!" RJ said through gritted teeth. "If Dad hears about this, he's going to be upset. He's not going to want everyone to think that we have a mouse problem in our building!"

"Even if you do," Rebekah said with a roll of her eyes at mouse.

"Sorry," Mouse squeaked out. Once everyone calmed down, the staff tried to fix up the lobby so that it looked like a spooky mansion again. Then someone called out.

"Where's Danny?"

Everyone got very quiet as they looked around the room.

"Danny? Danny Dakota?" the director shouted. Some of the staff began scouring the lobby.

"Where is he?" Dylan demanded. "We have a schedule to keep!"

After a few minutes of looking, Dylan sighed. "Well he's done it again, hasn't he?" he asked with a frown. "He did this last week too. We were signing autographs and he just disappeared so he could go to an ice cream shop!"

"Don't worry," one of the staff members said. "We'll find him."

"This is ridiculous," Dylan said with a huff.

"That's what happens when you work with kids," the director shrugged. "Take five everyone."

Rebekah, RJ, and Mouse grouped together. "Where do you think he went?" Rebekah asked.

"Well Dylan Banner said he slipped away to an ice cream shop before. We should go look for him," RJ suggested.

"Good idea!" Rebekah and Mouse agreed. They left the lobby of the apartment building and began walking up and down the block. There were a few little shops, like the pizza shop, the corner store and a small deli that had ice cream too. Rebekah, RJ and Mouse spent the whole day searching.

"Oh no, Mom's going to be here soon," Rebekah frowned as she glanced at her watch.

"Don't worry, I'm sure they'll find him," RJ said.

"I hope Hollywood didn't scare him off," Mouse murmured as he patted the top of Hollywood's head.

Chapter 6

When Rebekah's mother pulled up in front of the apartment building the kids were just walking back.

"How exciting," Rebekah's mother said when she saw all the cameras and trucks. "Did you get to meet Danny Dakota?" she asked.

"No," Rebekah said with a frown. "He disappeared before I could."

"Well go grab your things and say goodbye to RJ," her mother said. "Mouse's mother is waiting for him. It's a school night and you three need to get to bed."

Rebekah's mother left the van for a moment to say hello to RJ's parents. She didn't think she needed to lock it because she was still close by. Once Rebekah and Mouse had all of their things and said goodbye to RJ they hurried back to the van. They clamored in to the middle seat, still talking about the day.

"Mom you should have seen it," Rebekah said with a sigh. "Danny Dakota swung across the lobby! He does his own stunts! How cool is that?"

"I wouldn't exactly call it a stunt," Mouse pointed out with a frown.

"Well what you pulled sure was a stunt," Rebekah whispered to him.

Mouse frowned and tucked Hollywood back into his pocket. "I just hope it wasn't the reason Danny took off."

"Is it true that Danny Dakota is missing?" Rebekah's mother asked.

"It is," Mouse nodded. "But he's disappeared before."

"I'm sure he'll be fine," Rebekah's mother said. "Poor little guy probably just needed a break."

Chapter 7

That night after they dropped Mouse off at his house, Rebekah hurried into the house. She wanted to get on the computer to check and see if Danny had been found yet.

She was in such a hurry that she left her bag in the van. When she went to unpack it, she realized it was still in the van.

"Mom, I'm just going to grab my bag," she called out as she stepped out the front door. When she walked up to the van she realized she didn't have the keys. She tried the door just in case and was surprised to find it open.

She always locked the doors and her mother always double checked. Not only was it unlocked, but it was a little bit open, as if someone didn't know that it had to be slammed to be closed.

"Strange," Rebekah muttered. But she had been so excited about Danny Dakota that she figured she must have just forgotten to lock it and close it properly. She grabbed her bag, locked the door and slammed it shut.

Then she ran back into the house. She couldn't wait to get to school the next day and tell her friend Amanda about seeing Danny Dakota in person!

Chapter 8

Rebekah waited by her locker the next day. She knew that Amanda would want to hear all about Danny Dakota. Rebekah only wished she had more to tell. She had only seen him for a few minutes.

On the news this morning they said he was still missing, but no one was too concerned because he had a reputation for running off. That made Rebekah a little sad. She thought it would hurt her feelings if she went missing and no one was worried.

"Did you see him, did you see him?" Amanda asked as she hurried up to Rebekah's locker.

"I did," Rebekah said proudly. "I mean I didn't get to meet him or anything, but I was in the same lobby as him!" she giggled.

"How amazing," Amanda sighed dreamily. "I have such a crush on him!" she gushed.

"A crush?" Rebekah scrunched up her nose. "Ew!"

"Oh stop, you like him as much as I do!" Amanda rolled her eyes.

"No, ma'am," Rebekah shook her head firmly. "I respect his detective work. That's it!"

"You do know he's just an actor right Rebekah?" Amanda laughed.

"Well, I bet he likes to solve real mysteries too," Rebekah said with confidence. She knew a thing or two about solving mysteries and she was sure that Danny did too. As they walked to class Rebekah told Amanda about Hollywood escaping and Danny's disappearance.

"I hope he's okay," Amanda frowned.

"Me too," Rebekah nodded and opened the door to their classroom. When they walked in most of the other kids were already sitting at their desks.

One boy was sitting all the way in the back row with the hood of his sweatshirt pulled down over his head. Rebekah only noticed him because he was tapping his fingernails nervously on the desk. She wasn't sure who he was, which was strange, because she knew all of the kids in her class.

During the class she waited for the teacher to introduce the new student, but she never did. She didn't even seem to notice him in the back of the class. Rebekah found this very suspicious.

Chapter 9

When class was over, Rebekah waited until all of the other kids left the room. The boy was still sitting at his desk, as if he was waiting for her to leave. Rebekah fiddled with her book bag.

Finally the boy got up and walked out of the class. Rebekah waited a few moments and then followed after him.

As she suspected he walked to her next class. Just as before he took the desk all the way in the back. Once again her teacher didn't seem to notice him and didn't introduce him.

Rebekah raised her hand.

"Yes Rebekah?" Mr. Woods her science teacher asked.

"Mr. Woods aren't you going to-" she glanced over at the boy. He put his finger to his lips. Rebekah wasn't sure what to do. She wanted to know who he was, but she didn't really want to get him in trouble. "Give us our homework assignment?" Rebekah asked.

"Oh yes, thank you for reminding me," Mr. Woods laughed. "I almost forgot, can't have that!" All of the other kids in the class glared at Rebekah for making sure they had homework.

Rebekah was staring at the boy in the back of the class. When the bell rang Rebekah hung back, but this time the boy was one of the first ones to leave the classroom. Rebekah followed after him, but by the time she reached the hall he was gone.

"How strange," she whispered to herself. She was determined to find out who the boy was. She noticed Mouse at his locker.

"Mouse, there's this new boy in my classes and I can't figure out who he is," Rebekah said with a frown as she walked up beside him.

"Well have you asked him his name?" Mouse asked as he stacked up his books.

"Uh, no," Rebekah laughed a little. She hadn't even thought of just introducing herself.

"Well that's usually a good way to meet someone," Mouse winked at her. "Have to hurry," he said as he waved over his shoulder.

Chapter 10

Rebekah's next class was gym. She changed into her gym clothes and then joined her friend Jaden in some basketball before class started. As she was shooting the ball into the hoop she noticed someone staring at her from the bleachers.

When she looked up she saw the boy with the hood pulled up over his head. She was so distracted that when Jaden passed her the ball, it bounced right off the side of her head.

"Ouch!" she gasped and lost her balance. She fell hard on the gym floor.

"I'm so sorry!" she heard Jaden call. But when she opened her eyes, she was looking right up at Danny Dakota.

"Are you okay?" he asked her with a frown.

"I'm okay," she replied. She glanced over at Jaden to see if he saw Danny Dakota too, but when she looked back, Danny was gone. She blinked and sat up, rubbing her head.

"Rebekah I didn't mean it honest," Jaden said as he crouched down next to her.

"Did you see him?" Rebekah asked as she stared around the gym.

"See who?" Jaden wondered.

"Danny Dakota," Rebekah replied.

"The actor?" Jaden shook his head. "Maybe you need to see the nurse Rebekah."

"Maybe I do," she sighed.

Chapter 11

For the rest of the school day Rebekah searched for Danny Dakota. She didn't see the boy in the hooded sweatshirt at all. She even asked Mouse to look for him too.

"I'm sure it was Danny Dakota Mouse," she told him at lunch.

"And you had just been hit in the head with a basketball," Mouse reminded her with a frown.

"I know, I know," Rebekah sighed. "But I looked right at him. He asked me if I was okay!"

"Why would Danny Dakota ever come here?" Mouse asked with a shake of his head.

"I don't know, but think about it," Rebekah insisted. "He disappeared after Hollywood escaped. Mom left the van alone while she talked to RJ's parents. Then that night after I got home I went back out to get my bag and the door to the van was open!"

"That is odd," Mouse said. "But still, if you were a Hollywood star and you wanted to run away, would it be to school?" he asked with a grin.

"Probably not," Rebekah admitted. "It does seem strange. But I know what I saw," she said firmly.

"Well I'll help you look," Mouse said. "But don't get your hopes too high Rebekah, big stars like Danny Dakota don't disappear so they can go to school."

Even though Mouse and Rebekah looked everywhere for Danny, they couldn't find him. Rebekah didn't see the boy in the hooded shirt in any more of her classes.

She felt a little sad on the way home, but the more she thought about it, the more sure she was that she had seen Danny. He had looked right at her after all!

She knew she needed the help of another detective, so when she got home she called her cousin RJ.

"RJ," Rebekah said when he answered the phone. "Danny Dakota is here! He's in our town."

"What?" RJ asked with surprise. "Are you sure about that?"

"Yes I'm sure, I saw him at school today," Rebekah said quickly.

"At school? Why would Danny Dakota be at school?" he asked.

"I don't know, but that's where I saw him," Rebekah replied with certainty.

"Do you know where he is now?" RJ asked curiously. "Everyone is still looking for him. If you know where he is, you should probably tell someone."

"I don't know," Rebekah frowned. "I lost him after I got hit with a basketball."

"You were hit with a basketball?" RJ asked with surprise. Rebekah, did you really see him or did you just think you saw him?" RJ asked. "After all those episodes you watched he's probably stuck in your brain."

"I really saw him," Rebekah insisted. "You have to believe me RJ, I'm not making this up."

"I believe you Rebekah," RJ knew his younger cousin was one of the best detectives around. "Well what do you think he's doing there?" RJ asked with confusion. "Maybe he has amnesia and doesn't remember who he is?"

"Maybe," Rebekah sighed. "I just hope wherever he is, he has a safe place to stay."

Chapter 12

As the day got later, Rebekah got more worried about Danny. She knew he couldn't stay in the school all night because there were janitors and security guards.

She didn't think he'd have anywhere to be safe, or maybe even any food to eat. She sat down on her bed and tried to think about what she would do if she was hiding out and had no one to help her.

She would try to find a safe place where no one would look for her. Since kids are less likely to be suspicious, she would probably hide out where kids were instead of adults. The only places she could think that kids would be, were school and the playground.

Then she would probably want to be somewhere close to food. She remembered that there was a little store not far from the playground that sold all kinds of snacks and ice cream. If she was hiding out, she would definitely hide near the playground. But she would also need a place to sleep.

"Hm," she said thoughtfully. "I wouldn't be able to sleep on the swings and the slide would be pretty uncomfortable. Plus, what if it rained?" she tapped her chin for a moment. Then suddenly she knew exactly where Danny was. She grabbed her jacket.

"Mom, I'll be back before dark!" she called to her mother as she ran out the door. She ran all the way to Mouse's house and pounded on his door.

"Rebekah?" Mouse asked with surprise. "Why are you knocking so loudly?"

"I think I know where he is," Rebekah said with a wide smile. "Come on Mouse, let's go find him!"

"Where is he?" Mouse asked as he followed after Rebekah. "Are you sure you know where he is?"

"I'm sure," Rebekah said with confidence. "Follow me!"

She led Mouse to the park, which was mostly empty as it was getting dark. She walked across the open field to the trees.

"Rebekah, where are you going?" Mouse asked as he followed after her. "I don't think a television star is going to be hiding out in the trees."

"Maybe not in the trees," Rebekah said in a whisper as she stopped in front of the tree house where Mouse held meetings of his secret club. "Maybe in a tree house," she pointed up to the tree house where a small light was shining. Mouse's eyes widened.

"Do you really think he's up there?" he asked.

"Only one way to find out," Rebekah replied and began climbing up the rope ladder to the tree house. When she reached the top and peeked over the edge, she spotted what was making the light. There was a flashlight on the table in the middle of the tree house.

Chapter 13

"Hello?" Rebekah called out as she climbed the rest of the way up into the tree house. "Is anyone up here?"

"Go away!" a muffled voice shouted back from the corner of the tree house.

Mouse climbed up right behind Rebekah.

"We're not going anywhere," Mouse said firmly. "You're trespassing."

"Go away!" the voice shouted again. Mouse ducked his head and tried to see through the shadows into the corner. When he leaned over, the mouse in his pocket slipped out. It ran across the floor of the tree house.

"Hollywood!" Mouse said with a frown.

"Ah! What's that?" the voice cried out as the mouse ran toward the corner. "Is that a mouse? A real mouse?" the voice demanded.

"It's okay, he won't hurt you," Rebekah promised him as she scooped up the small white mouse. "He's a nice mouse," she added as she handed Mouse's pet back to him. "Now, what are you doing up here all alone?" she asked the boy huddled in the corner.

"That's just it, I want to be alone," the boy replied. "Please go away."

"I'm sorry, I can't do that Danny," Rebekah said with a shake of her head.

"Why not?" Danny asked in a growl.

"Because it's not safe for you to sleep in this tree house," Rebekah insisted. "Even if you are Danny Dakota."

"You know who I am?" Danny gasped with surprise. "Did you tell anyone? Any reporters?"

"No reporters," Rebekah shook her head. "Only my cousin and my friend Mouse here know who you are."

"Oh good," Danny sighed. "But I guess you're going to tell, huh?"

"I won't tell anyone," Rebekah promised. "If you tell me why you're hiding out like this."

"The truth is, I needed a break," Danny said. "I just wanted to be a normal kid for a few days."

"Well then you're in the wrong tree house," Mouse laughed.

"I'm sorry, I've never had the chance to go to a real school," Danny explained with a shake of his head. "I've been working in television for so long that sometimes I forget what it's like to just be a kid," he frowned as he looked at them.

"Well we can change that," Rebekah said with a smile. "But you can't sleep in a tree house."

"He can sleep at my house," Mouse offered. "Then we can all go to school together tomorrow."

"I think that's a great idea," Rebekah agreed. "What do you think Danny?"

Danny smiled and nodded. "Sounds good to me. I can't wait to go to school again!"

Chapter 14

The next day at school Rebekah and Mouse showed Danny all the fun things about being in school and some of the not so fun things. Danny had a great time meeting their friends, even Amanda, who nearly fainted when she saw him.

They all promised to keep his secret. But by the end of the day, Danny was worn out.

"I don't know how you do this every day," he laughed as he looked at the stack of homework he'd been given. "School might be a lot of fun, but it's a lot of work too."

"Well Danny if you want to stay, we can help you stay," Rebekah offered with a smile.

"It's been great," Danny admitted. "But my fans are looking forward to that new movie."

"Yes we are!" Rebekah said happily.

"So I better get back to work," he sighed. He pulled out his cell phone to call for his agent to come pick him up. "Thanks guys for showing me what it's like to be a normal kid."

"Normal?" Mouse raised an eyebrow.

Danny laughed. "This is one adventure I won't ever forget."

"Just remember," Rebekah said as she walked him out of the school. "If you decide to base a character in your movie or television show on me, it's Rebekah with a 'k' and you can leave out the whole basketball hitting me in the head part."

"You got it, Rebekah," he smiled and shook her hand. "I'll make sure you all have passes to the premier of the movie."

"Thanks Danny!" Rebekah waved to him as he climbed into his agent's car. She was happy to have met him and even happier that she knew just what it was like to be a normal kid. Well, a normal kid that was also a detective, of course.

Next Steps

I really hope that you've enjoyed this collection of stories and I'd love to hear from you at the Facebook page below - please do stop by and let us know how you are enjoying the books!

Rebekah - Girl Detective:
http://www.facebook.com/RebekahGirlDetective

I very much appreciate your reviews and comments so thank you in advance for taking a moment to leave one for "Rebekah - Girl Detective: Books 9-16."

Sincerely,
PJ Ryan

Visit the author website for a complete list of all titles available.

PJRyanBooks.com

Now Available in Audio

Several of the PJ Ryan titles are now available as audiobooks!

Visit the author website for a complete list at:
PJRyanBooks.com

You can also listen to free audio samples there.

Titles by PJ Ryan Can be Found Here

PJRyanBooks.com
*Visit the author page to save big on special bundled sets!

****

"Rebekah - Girl Detective"

#1 The Mysterious Garden
#2 Alien Invasion
#3 Magellan Goes Missing
#4 Ghost Hunting
#5 Grown-Ups Out To Get Us?!
#6: The Missing Gems
#7: Swimming With Sharks?!
#8: Magic Gone Wrong!
#9: Mystery At Summer Camp
#10: Zombie Burgers
#11: Mouse's Secret
#12: The Missing Ice Cream
#13: The Ghost Snowman
#14: Monkey Business
#15: Science Magic
#16: Quiet On The Set!

"RJ - Boy Detective"

#1: The Mysterious Crate
#2: Vampire Hunting
#3: Alien Goo!
#4: Mystery Poo
#5: Mr. Pip Is Missing!
#6: Where Is Hensely?
#7: Night Noises
#8: The Cheese Thief

Made in United States
Orlando, FL
14 December 2021

11747374R00137